"Ursula Holden: remember her name. Buy her books and you will buy magic."

—Susan Hinerfeld
Los Angeles Times

"To put it calmly, as she might herself, Ursula Holden is an unusual novelist. I strongly advise you to try her."

—Walter Clemons
Newsweek

"When all the familiar tests have been applied —the economy, the individual way of handling dialogue, the tension without strain—there is always, with writing as good and original as this, an extra and overriding quality harder to define. . . . The best single word for it is organic."

—*The Guardian*

The Cloud Catchers

URSULA HOLDEN

PINNACLE BOOKS   NEW YORK

The author and the publisher wish to thank
Kalmann Music, Inc.
for permission to reprint lyrics from
"Let's Twist Again,"
© *Kalmann Music, Inc. 1961.*

THE CLOUD CATCHERS

A Pinnacle Books edition, published by special arrangement with Methuen, Inc.

First printing, March 1981

ISBN: 0-523-41272-X

Cover photograph by Brian Leng

Printed in the United States of America

PINNACLE BOOKS, INC.
1430 Broadway
New York, New York 10018

'Twas but my tongue, 'twas not my soul that swore.

EURIPIDES

They're only young once. You can't blame them. Demons for hot water, both of them. Demons. They'll have their skins ruined."

My mother excused Eileen and me to my father, who had always been tightfisted with money, complaining of bills, a taciturn man. He rarely spoke to us girls. Them and Us, two camps under the one roof, with my mother the mediator when necessary. Washing was almost our only luxury. We'd wash in the outhouse. In summer the boiler was never lit; we washed from kettles heated on the gas, heaving them into the sink, having first removed the hens' buckets. The stone of the shallow sink was in a cracked state from the heavy buckets used for the hens' mash. Our plumbing was elementary. The outhouse had been a dairy once, the farm a going concern, before my mother married. Different now. Eileen and I didn't worry about the chipped sink. You could sit on the wooden drainboard, the slime in the grooves hardened with age, and dip your feet. There was just room in it to crouch. We didn't mind grease or damp, the outhouse was companionable. It had a tin roof, noisy in wet weather or when birds hopped on it. After downpours of rain the water seeped up the step and over the floor. "Lord God Lord, bad drainage has us

1

ruined," moaned my mother. Eileen and I thought the outhouse the best room, we liked the bath under the wooden top, which had a waste pipe but no tap. The cover hadn't been removed in my memory. My mother kept the delft, bags of meal, flatirons, and culinary objects on the wooden top.

We weren't house-proud. My mother called me her own right hand, she could rely on my helping. My cousin Eileen did nothing. I wanted my parents to be proud of me, like the parents of the girls at college who lived in grand houses near to the city. Carpets, porcelain fittings, garages, were not in our scheme of things. I was the only girl in my class at the convent to get a place at the college. I couldn't invite the other students. The covered cobwebby bath, the concrete floor and cracked sink, the lavatory out in the yard, precluded it. My mother said privies were healthier.

Eileen, being only a cousin, not born to it, complained sometimes in bad weather. She'd come to live with us when small. I liked to think she was my truest friend, dependent on me, but she preferred Bridie, the chemist's daughter. We not only washed ourselves and our clothes in the outhouse, Eileen and I sometimes took our meals there. My parents didn't seem to notice. In addition to our washing habits and the gas we used, my father grumbled about grocery bills. My mother's hands were wrinkly from hard work. Hens made a lot of work; eggs were our standby. If a hen got old, past laying, a boiler made a Sunday treat, otherwise our meals were usually eggs in some form or other. Boiling scraps, adding bran meal to the buckets, was a daily chore; the sink was the easiest place for the buckets.

When Eileen was fifteen she'd had enough of the convent, no further education for her, leave the village,

2

find somewhere better, the city, England possibly, forget my parents who had reared her, forget poverty and scrimping, make for the razzle-dazzle. Her real mother, my London aunt, hadn't wanted her, which didn't bother Eileen. Being unwanted gave her a hard confidence. The village women whispered about her origin, about how she carried on. Eileen felt no loyalty or obligation, she used people as she might use stepping-stones, to move to better things. She said I was a mug, going to college when the razzle-dazzle world waited. My father appeared to prefer her. Lack of a father didn't concern Eileen, let the world talk.

I was ashamed of my father's job. At college your father's job mattered, as did your home. I let on he was a manager instead of a clerk in a menswear shop in the local town. Too old for promotion, he was an embittered man. My mother told me in a moment of confidence that my grandparents would toss in their graves if they knew how their girls had ended. They'd planned travel for my mother and my aunt, and secure marriages. It hadn't happened. A dour menswear-selling husband got my mother. Aunt disappeared. The grandparents died, my father moved into the old farm with my mother, let it go to rack. For her sake I wanted to be a teacher. I don't think she cared deeply what I did.

"Are you at your washing again?"

It was my father at the outhouse door. The front door stuck. We used the back. He'd opened the door ajar for his wheezy voice to be heard. He'd known I would be washing. Why hadn't I waited for Eileen? Inside I'd known he'd come there, watch me alone, that his voice, his excited breathing, would sound at the door before she came. I'd lifted the hens' buckets down, arranged towels round the drainboard for a soft seat.

3

I'd filled the sink with hot water, not waiting for Eileen to get back.

"Don't come. Not yet. Don't come in."

He pushed the door, stood there, his cycling clips still round his lower calves. Had Eileen been with me we'd have grinned, not minding, like a kind of game. We laughed at his black cycling clips, his sorry little eyes, his moustache with the hanging points, his breathing. He was bald. His eyes, when he watched us wash, changed. We laughed because he left his bike under the thornbush at the station, ashamed of owning no car to drive to the town, ashamed of taking sandwiches. I couldn't laugh now, Eileen wasn't there.

"Washing? At your washing still?"

"I'm off to the dance."

I hugged my knees up, leaning my hair over. My legs where they'd touched the bare drainboard had a sour smell, like old herrings. Years of making mash had permeated the stone and wood, no scouring could remove it. We didn't mind.

"Dancing again? Yourselves and your pleasures. Where is your cousin?"

He rarely used our names, preferring "your cousin," "your mother," or "herself." Mostly he stayed silent. He rubbed one shoe against his cycle clip, the metal rasping against the cloth.

"She'll be here any minute."

I'd be all right then, I could dress, move from the sink when Eileen came. With Eileen the outhouse was a bright, safe place, where we could sing, practice our dancing steps, laugh. Eileen mimicked my father, mocking his breathing, the smell of his clothes, which she thought worse than the buckets or the powder my

4

mother rubbed into the hens' feathers to kill mites. Why hadn't I waited? I ducked lower. Why didn't he go?

"We're modest, now we're getting the grand education."

He sniffed. He resented my place at the college. When I passed the entrance exam his eyes had looked frightened, afraid that I'd earn more than he did one day. Self-shame made him contemptuous of others. Why should a girl be educated? The lads had to provide in the end. Wasn't he the man to know? He'd been pleased when Eileen said no to a college education. She'd been writing away to firms in the city and to England, had gone now to waylay the postman. Hurry, Eileen.

"I was lucky getting a place. Eileen could have passed easily, had she tried."

I didn't enjoy college. I'd two years to go. Being different, being poor, made it more difficult. My father lowered his weak chin, a sorry older bird of a man, on one leg, rubbing his cycle clip. He said Eileen was wiser to go and earn wages. Aye. Fuel cost good cash, and all that washing, to say nothing of the food for the table. Had I considered the price of food? Then there was furniture, a home was costly. I looked round. In twenty years nothing had been replaced or mended, and he knew it. He knew we sneered at him, sneered at his appearance, his job and poorly fitting teeth. He had grown to accept Eileen, child of my mother's sister, who sent nothing for her keep.

I squeezed water from my flannel. I'd not move till he left, until he went through into the living room. We ate chocolate in the outhouse and read magazines. My Mars bar had got splashed, soap had soaked into a puddle on my open page. Towels hung from rusty hooks.

The dirtied pots, the paraphernalia of hens, were strewn about.

"We don't buy new furniture. It's not palatial here, is it? Some of the girls have open-planned houses."

"Open plan? What's them? What's them things?"

"Which things?"

"Them two yolks."

He put his hand out, touched me. I hunched back, sick. He'd never touched before. Hurry, Eileen.

"Eve. Eve. Is it your father? Is your father back?"

My mother's voice called faintly from the bedroom. She lay there each day until tea, for two hours or more. She had a carrying voice, not breathy like my father, she'd only to whisper and the hens heard, running to her for food.

In the old days when my mother was Protestant, her family had respect locally. The village used to defer to my grandparents, the only resident non-Catholics, affluent and strange, equal almost to the priest and the doctor. Then, when my mother married, things changed. The first to change had been her religion, changed for my father. Change in the property had been more gradual. My father had not bothered with the farm, had sold the herd, sold off the land or let it for grazing. The hens were kept for my mother's sake. It was said in the village that the luck of the farm died when my mother turned Catholic, trying to become one with the community like her husband. To make it worse, we were not good Catholics, members in name only. Failure in practice made us more than ever censored. My mother excused herself for reasons of fatigue. My father had his bronchitis. Eileen and I, once we'd left Mother Perpetua at the convent, were too busy. Our hair, our reading, dancing, were more important. We had our futures,

6

real and imaginary, to plan. We didn't believe. We none of us cared for religion; hating it was a common bond. Eileen said that my mother's beads, my father's mumblings, were put on, an excuse.

Eileen learned lots from her magazines, English ones, sent by her real mother. The only consistent support from my London aunt was magazines, coming in place of checks. Eileen believed that an advice column from across the Irish Sea taught you more than a hundred books. A concerned reply to troubles was better than a mother's care. She showed no interest in her real mother, magazines were best. We liked the illustrations. My mother read these books too, though sometimes she thought them shocking. Questionable literature from an aunt who'd gone for good was another bond. My father sucked his top teeth down, looking at them. My mother once told me that she'd dreamed of being thin, of marrying a man like Paul Getty to fly her about the world. Instead she'd stayed in her own village, in her own old home. She'd like Eileen and me to have a different life.

"Is herself in the bed? Aye, there again." He pulled back his hand at the sound of her calling. My skin felt burned.

"She is tired. Maxie has been . . . bad." I tried to keep my voice calm, to stay unhurried. I swallowed the taste in my mouth. He'd touched. Hurry, Eileen.

"Hmph."

At fifteen my brother Maxie had to be lifted, spoonfed, cleaned, was too much for one person. Eileen was supposed to take turns helping. She was selfish, doing the minimum. On Saturdays, the night of the dance, she'd go to lengths to avoid it. This was my Saturday to go out. She would argue that Maxie was not *her* brother, a cousin only, not worth sacrificing a life for, not worth a second of it. She did what suited her. Maxie didn't recognize anyone, didn't count, she had her own future. I tried to breathe calmly. My father never mentioned Maxie, or that he had a son. He bent now to remove his clips, putting his shoe on the bath top. He glanced over his arm. I had the towel round now, I felt braver. He knew I'd minded.

Then I heard Eileen. I heard quick footsteps, heard her pull the latch. Since it got broken, the handle had a piece of plaited string. She kicked the door panel as my father moved into the house, softly closing the living-room door. I longed to be like Eileen, kicking at doors, with lipstick slashed carelessly and letters in my hand. One tooth was smudged with rose madder, a frizzed curl poked into her eye. I sat depending on her in shallow, lukewarm water.

"I got word. From the gas people."

"Will you go, Eileen? Don't go. What do they say?"

"I'll go surely. They've vacancies. They don't insist on knowledge of Irish."

"Eileen, don't."

"Why are you red? You've been blushing."

"I am not."

"You're redder than a pig. Has he been at it? Old goat, up to his tricks."

"No, no."

"He has. Don't kid me, kid. Look at you. Red."

"No, Eileen."

"Liar. Get your bra on. Your bust is worse than the Queen of England's."

"Mammy is upstairs still. Her head is bad."

"I'm not surprised. Did you hear them last night? At it like animals."

8

"What do you mean? They're too old."

"Don't kid me, kid. This whole house is an affliction. I'm off to the razzle-dazzle."

I hated her ingratitude. Her real mother had done nothing, she owed us everything. She thought only of razzle-dazzle, New York, Paris. Ireland had no razzle-dazzle. She said few women but the Irish would endure it. Marriage here was a trap. Even the old rooster had shown more kindness to the hens than my father had. She'd laugh if he rode his bike under a train. Oven roasting was too good for his kind. The rooster, a cruel bird, had died early of an unknown cause. He trod the hens, woke them and our family each day, then he was found dead. My mother cried, though he was no real loss, apart from fertilizing hens. His swelled red claws kicked out at feeding time, pecking your wrists and ankles when food was put down, insisting on first grab, not letting the rest near, striking with his beak. My mother had found him, had wept over his stiff-stretched legs, his gaping beak. She'd settled his wings neatly, had dug his grave, splashing her peck-marked wrists with tears. It had been springtime then. Blossoms from the apple tree fell over the grave. We gathered some into a little heap. I cried too. I had a pet hen, Biddy, who stayed apart from the rest, different. Neither the rooster nor my father were great on cleanliness. My father washed the parts of him that showed to customers, hands, neck, face, and bald head, a "light sluice" in the outhouse. The rooster's feathers had been dirty from dust baths.

"I think he is saddened over Maxie. He doesn't show his feelings."

"He has none. Mad goat. Don't kid me, kid. He shows us his feelings in here."

9

I thought that there must have been a time before Maxie was diagnosed hopeless, before the General Hospital gave the final verdict, when my father must have been ambitious for him. Plans for his son, a career in mind, accounting perhaps, something in the veterinary line, a boy to boast about instead of not mentioning. Once my father must have looked young, with a mouse-colored moustache, hair on his head, real teeth. His present set clicked onto his tongue each night behind his newspaper. His scalp was marked now over the ears, from the rim of his cap. He read all evening, ignoring the noise of Maxie, who slept off the living room in the old parlor. Each evening was the same, the rustling of the pages, my father's teeth, and Maxie. Because of Maxie my mother looked fifty instead of forty. Because of him my father lost faith in all doctors. We'd lost our religious faith. Coping had sapped us in many ways. Apart from bronchitic powders bought locally, my father did nothing about his chest.

We heard the privy chain. He'd gone round, along the side of the house by the hawthorn hedge where the path was green still from winter damp, in spite of months of drought. The water barrel in the yard was dry now but for sludge. Mosquitoes bred. There'd been no rain since March. We flushed only when necessary. Watch out, Eileen said. The mad goat must have done his business, he'd come through the outhouse. Not that she cared, she was going out.

"Out? But it's my turn, it's my Saturday. I've stayed for two running."

"Try stopping me."

She stuck her tongue out, at me first, then in the direction of the footsteps, crossing the way they'd come, retracing the greened pathway. Eileen wasn't pretty, her mousy curls were bleached into streaks round her square jaw. Her front teeth stuck out a bit, but her self-confidence was infectious, she believed she was ravishing. The local laddos thought her more beautiful than Bridie, because she thought so. Bridie had real beauty. Sometimes Eileen got spots.

"You're not to go, Eileen."

"Don't fret. You'll not be burdened with me long. I'll be no martyr for a vegetable. Look at my aunt. Real old, that's all it's done for her."

"Mammy loves Maxie."

"Love? Don't kid me. If that's love, keep it."

Eileen had the letter that she longed for, she had my blouse on, unworn yet. I envied her tough ways. I picked the chocolate up, fit only for the bucket. My father would be settled behind his newspaper, to click his teeth, pick at his eyebrows for the evening. Maxie's noise would increase until he got fed. I'd known inside me that I'd not get out. The hooks of my bra cut into my back. My mother called again.

Maxie had medicine to tone him down. When he got really hungry he sounded like a gobbling animal. He gobbled with his tongue against his throat, between banshee shrieks. The hens started, they too knew the time, clucking imperiously for grain. Maxie, my father, the hens made their noises for attention. The only quiet one was Biddy, my pet hen, who never developed properly, had never laid an egg, nor did she fight for food or mingle. My mother said she wasn't worth her keep. I loved her. I worried about my mother getting fatigued. If anything happened, my father would be useless. My mother called me pet names when she wanted favors. She resembled Eileen, large-hipped, same shape hands, shriveled from hard work now. Old snapshots showed

11

her like Eileen, looking up under the apple tree branches with a young expectant face, her life ahead of her, promising. Now, older, uglier, her life was disappointing. The same house for her, awful plumbing, patched gutters, decay. It needed rewiring, the window wood was rotten, there were worms in the furniture. We ate almost nothing but eggs, brown, white, and speckled.

My mother thought that Eileen's hardness resulted from rejection by her real mother. Still, hard-skinned folk prospered. I could hear Eileen above, humming, painting her already bright face. She did this quickly, often without a mirror. She'd not told her news to my parents, not spoken. She wouldn't wait for tea, she'd go to Bridie's. Bridie was under Eileen's spell too. Her house was nice, best in the village, with good food. Bridie had spent time in France. Eileen picked up a few French expressions from her. I heard shoes being kicked about overhead. *"Mais oui, madame. Mais oui, madame, que vous avez un beau bébé."* Bridie didn't dance well, she wasn't clever, except at French. That was the summer of the twist. We practiced constantly, to dazzle the laddos at the dances. Eileen and I were best, had learned it first. Young people came from outlying parts, in buses to the next village, where the station was. We shared the same church and convent. The priest involved himself in the fun, concerned because the young of the district left after they'd finished school, the same as Eileen, looking for the bright lights. The district lacked vitality. A longing to escape came over the laddos and girls once out of the clutches of Mother Perpetua. The priest did his best. The older women whispered. His dances were depraved, that twist dance was immoral. He'd been known to join in, twisting his limbs in movements unsuitable to a man in a

12

cassock. I lived for the dances. Earlier that summer, I'd met Matthew, on holiday from England. We'd met only the one time.

Eileen was coming down again, mouth shining dark, her selfish ready-for-the-dance face smirking. She wore pink pointy shoes to match the blouse. Her skirt wrinkled over her round thighs.

"Please, Eileen, stay."

"Please, nothing. Do what you want with *your* life. This may be my last village hop. I'm off. You tend the vegetable. Toodle-oo."

I pictured her dancing across the country, skirt clinging to her big bottom, pausing at lighted cities to smile her painted smile at likely laddos, dancing onward, her smile brightening as cities got brighter. Onward, over the Channel, spiraling, dissatisfied, stopping at the megalopolis, real razzle-dazzle, and her real mother. She'd forget the long hot summer, forget the feeding hens, forget twisting. She'd never loved my parents, said what she thought about them and Maxie. We used to love dancing in our white skirts under the apple blossoms, the white hens moving after the grain as we flung it, lifting their scaly legs. The grain would hit the apple trunk and them, added fun.

It was under the big apple tree that Matthew had kissed me, where the cockerel lay buried. He'd come there, one of a busload of strangers for the dance, dancing sophisticatedly, saying the twist was outmoded where he came from, had stayed all evening with me, walking me home later, his plump soft face bending to kiss mine, saying he was a dentist. I'd lovely teeth, such teeth would put him out of business, he liked every bit of me. He whispered lovingly under the apple tree, enfolding me with toothpaste-smelling embraces. I was his

13

destiny, his certain star, he believed now that real colleens existed. Were my eyes real? I was to wait until August when he'd come again. He'd write. I was miraculous. He'd make further plans, wait. Trust him. It was September now. I'd not told anyone. Eileen would jeer. Both she and Bridie scoffed at love. Break hearts, keep your own whole. Love was a joke. But I believed Matthew. Those pleasant eyes surely had meant it. There was a reason for not writing.

I washed and fed Maxie, thinking of Eileen twisting, breaking the last of the village laddos' hearts, shy ones with temperance badges, eschewing alcohol to boost courage. Matthew hadn't been shy, had looked eye to eye at me, dancing recklessly with me. His jacket had smelled clinical, a bit like Listerine. "Be there. See you next August, don't change." He'd put my address in a special book. I didn't say I had a cousin or a handicapped brother in his bed, or that my home was sorry. We'd kissed more than we'd talked. I was the high spot of his holiday, he'd said, pushing me again against the rough tree bark. I pretended to be like Eileen, experienced at kissing, tried to forget the cock's bones under our feet, our house, our poverty, trying to think only of what to do with my tongue. Eileen often heard from holiday boys, throwing the letters away, scoffing. My mother complained that hens couldn't eat paper, not in the hens' buckets, please. Cruel Eileen. I pined and I yearned for one letter.

Attending to Maxie was disgusting. I minded it far more than Eileen, who made jokes. We had to rub his twisted limbs with liniment. Eileem laughed, singing and splashing his water, careless about everything. She rubbed mauve paste carelessly round her eyes before jazzing outside. She mixed lipstick with powder, she

14

never ironed her clothes. She took my things, wasn't above taking money from my mother's purse, for makeup or more magazines. She once took three pounds for a pearl choker. I found it under the apple tree, forgotten after one of her Saturdays. My mother didn't mention the stealing. Eileen made her laugh. Laughing was one of my mother's few pleasures, her sniggering becoming squeals, louder. Eileen took what she fancied, sweets, knickknacks, raisins. Occasionally we shared our clothes. The magazines were risky to leave about if the priest called. He had standards, though he was liberal. The church was strict about reading matter, literature could corrupt. My mother read them curled into her afternoon blankets. My father would click his teeth over a bikini advertisement. The books would end up, well read, curled at the edges, under Maxie's bottom, extra protection.

"You're very cruel and hard, Eileen."

"Mais oui. And a very *bon soir* to you."

Soon she would crash the outhouse door behind her, running over the yard to the privy before joining Bridie. Bridie was the only child of the Killems, who owned the chemist shop as well as the best home. They were ambitious for Bridie, denied her nothing. Though Bridie was rich, she liked our home. Contrast, a damp-greened yard, a privy with a broken chain, a tree with fruit that didn't sweeten—all had appeal, it was romantic. Her own house was compact, the walls plastered against wet, with lead-paned windows, a garage. Rooms were well heated. Bridie thought Eileen wonderful, copying her contempt of country things, kicking at wild flowers, uninterested in animals. She had to go to Mass, though.

I loved flowers, the apple and the hawthorn petals, frail in wet weather, the fuchsia in bloom now in the sun, shrubs of it by our gate. Eileen had sniggered when the cockerel died, refusing to help with the grave, kicking the blossoms we arranged. She thought we needed a few more deaths. She had no time for the sickly or dreary. Anyone sick or abnormal should be put down. Each day when I got home from college I checked that Biddy was alive. Mostly she stayed in a dirt patch during those summer days, unlike the adventurous hens, which sometimes flew up into the lower apple branches, perching like puffed flower bunches.

One autumn my mother made jelly from sour apples, the pink color looking nice on butter, shiny. White and red were my best colors. Before Matthew left me, he picked a fuchsia spray. That's how he'd remember me, a colleen wearing fuchsia flowers. I'd kept the flowers, touching them because he'd touched them, kissing, pressing until they fell in scraps. I loved May blossoms too. I had been looking at mayflowers stirred by the wind, smelling them, when they'd brought Maxie back, officially termed incurable. They had a bitter smell, unlike the fuchsia. Matthew's dentist's fingers had broken the spray neatly, telling me that London didn't have innocent girls, special girls like me. I was to stay as I was, a girl in a white skirt with white shoes. He'd kissed me again, whispering in his lovely accent while I worried about technique. A too-large nose could ruin a kiss, or a runny one. I was a bit unsure about babies. Eileen and Bridie knew. Apart from tending Maxie, physical contact was nearly unknown in our house, nor did we touch when dancing. I would have liked to kiss my mother sometimes. I don't think Eileen was right about my parents' noises at night; it was bronchitis.

"Don't be noisy, Eileen, when you get back. I worry about Mammy."

"Noise, noise. Is that all you can think of? This is a house of noise and madness. How long was the mad goat watching?"

"Don't say that."

And I was afraid, afraid of my father, afraid of life. It was more than madness or noise, it was a house of sadness. Laboring over Maxie, helping my mother, was a kind of insurance, helping to ward off sadness. What scared me made Eileen giggle, run. Once when the priest visited, she hid under Maxie's bed, her knuckles stuffed into her mouth, to copy him later, her painted mouth opening and shutting in priestly eloquence. Wasn't Maxie the grand fellow? Why, in no time he'd be at his books, and serving at the altar. Poor gobbling Maxie was the only religious observer in the family, the priest coming unasked. Eileen said the priest wasn't right either, to speak so.

"You're all mad in the head. Thanks be I'm not one of you. Mad buggers. I'll be gone soon."

"Don't kick your shoes about."

"You don't want to hear more like last night, that's what you mean. It's well Aunt isn't any younger."

"What do you mean?"

"Think of a row of Maxies in the old parlor. Toodle-oo."

She went then. Mammy called out again. My father hadn't answered her. He shuffled his paper, clicked his teeth. Maxie got noisier. The bed upstairs creaked as my mother put her legs over to the floor. I stared out at the flowers, white in the green, thinking of Matthew. I lifted the heavy buckets. Hens first, then the tea, then help my mother with Maxie. I'd go out later, smell the hawthorn, strongest in the dark. *Mais oui, madame. Mais oui, madame, que vous avez un beau bébé.*

17

Maxie never ate a lot. A finger of bread dipped into egg yolk, a little arrowroot, a slice of orange was enough. He liked spitting back into the face of the one who fed him. Eileen, out dancing, was avoiding being spat at. Though she had the nerve to spit back at him if he did it. My mother bought special oranges for Maxie, for squeezing. Idle Eileen got called "dotey" and "love" by my mother. Sacrifice didn't ensure gratitude, my mother took me for granted. Eileen didn't need love. I swallowed. Maxie smelled, no matter how much he got washed. No matter how little he ate, he got heavier, his limbs thickened, showing no sign of wasting. The doctor didn't come now, only the priest. Eileen warned my mother to watch out, Maxie might attack, keep out of range of his sickbed. He might try to ravish us. Hide, when the priest came. No soap disguised the smell of sickness long. I tried to ignore his noisy lips, his tongue lolling in and out, putting small bits on the spoon. I tried to forget Eileen, twisting in my blouse, smelling of lavender, with stolen makeup on her face. She and Bridie, the looker and the rich girl, were used to being ogled by laddos, desired from narrow beds all over the county. Eileen and Bridie had firm ideas. Catch a Lord Right, catch someone with cash and the right looks,

18

don't mind love. Eileen was going to places of opportunity, haunts of Lord Rights. A crumbled sprig of fuchsia, the promise of a letter, the memory of a kiss, didn't amount to much.

I envied Eileen. She was a burlesque, could twist her square face like the priest's, could depict the rolling of Maxie's eyes, my father's stare. If she had to help with Maxie, she stood back as far as possible. She'd tried throwing his pills into his mouth from a safe distance, a bull's-eye if she scored. My mother giggled, said no. Let Eve give him the pills. Eileen was a hard case. The night pills knocked him out. The day ones kept him manageable until mealtimes. He started when the hens did, his large nose breathing less quietly, loud, getting louder until he got breakfast. Meals calmed him. Better that Eve give the pills, my mother said, or they'd get lost round the place, rolling away. Eileen dancing, Eileen throwing pills, Eileen pulling faces wasn't so suitable a nurse. My mother laughed easily, tears of mirth usually shone in the corners of her eyes, the start or the end of an attack of mirth. Best that Eileen didn't tend Maxie, or excite him further. She'd also found Eileen snatching his feeding cup from him. Demon. Eileen's own cousin stricken by an unnamed condition, made to go thirsty. She had to turn her face from Eileen, not to show her smile. The bold demon girl had no pity.

My mother loved to see us dance. She understood, remembering when she'd danced herself, remembering the compulsion to roll the hips, to revolve repeatedly. Dancing was a joy, she didn't think it rude, high spirits needed to be released, though it was a pity to shock Miss Taylor in broad daylight. Eileen danced in the village street. Miss Taylor, the fattest of the village gossips, thought it sinful, showing the legs wantonly, it should be banned like rude literature. Miss Taylor made clothes. She wouldn't cut a skirt above knee level. The church ought not to modernize nuns' habits. Tradition, custom should stay unbroken. Led by Miss Taylor, the fat women murmured about the priest and bad dances, they murmured about young girls, particularly Eileen Joyne and Bridie Killem. My mother was blamed, she'd reaped a poor harvest, why else had she Maxie? A man could be forgiven, a man had the beasts to attend to, a hangover to ease, could more readily be excused from Mass. But, as the mother of God ruled heaven, so mothers ruled the home, so they should set an example. The priest coming to see Maxie was not enough. Our house was doomed. The General Hospital gave Maxie three years of possible life; thirteen had passed since. It wasn't surprising that my mother loved to rest in bed, liked an excuse for giggling, clapping her hand over her mouth so often, not to disgrace herself. If Eileen left, my mother might turn more to me for her enjoyment. One demon, me, instead of two. I'd get the pet names, all the laughter. I could teach her to twist, perhaps.

I scraped the arrowroot from the feeding cup. Strong light made Maxie restless. Once we'd tried laying him outside, out on the grass for his benefit in front of his own window. He lay, squinting with half-lunatic eyes at the fuchsia flowers, my flowers. I didn't want him seen. The yard would have been better, or the orchard with the hens. The village children hung over our gate, pointing their fingers, grinning. Was he human or a big rag doll? The sun had burned his skin. That, and the staring, decided it. A mistake, he'd stay inside in the future, unseen. He could see out from his bed, if indeed he saw anything.

20

My bedroom faced the back. I faced onto white apple blossoms, white hen feathers, white hawthorn. The hens' legs were like yellow stamens. In olden times, when my grandparents lived, there had been stables, a barn with a hayloft, for a thriving herd, cows, pigs, and a horse. Gone now, but for a rotting henhouse. Rain landed on the backs of the hens, dripping through holes in the corrugated sheeting above their heads. In a corner of the orchard had been a greenhouse, now only a mess of scrap iron, with a few pieces of glass tangled with nettles and sorrel leaves. No sign of the sties. We had none of the land. Everything had worsened, had worsened more quickly after Maxie came home for good. My father never spoke about the village people or his job, stuck to his paper. He sold ties, a scarf sometimes to a less important customer, but he was a jack-of-all-trades, making the tea and cleaning. With Eileen away, once her painted face was gone for good, his wages would be less threatened, he might be less pathetic. Maxie always looked sad, worse than the Duke of Windsor. After the wettest winter in living memory, we'd had the warmest summer. Perhaps it was the wet that caused the rooster's feet to swell. I rubbed Maxie's calves with special soap from Mr. Killem. He was generous, sending things for Maxie. We all liked lavender, it lingered a little on the hands.

"Managing all right, Eve?" my mother called from the outhouse, giving her face a rub with a damp towel. She and my aunt had been close once, as Eileen and I had been, now Aunt was never mentioned. The fat women whispered that Aunt had been wild, no wonder about Eileen, like followed like. Aunt left for another land, that was her end. Miss Taylor whispered this and other things to the fat ones. I would have liked to be able to put a face to the sender of the magazines. At Christmas, cards came. "Hope all is well. Comps of the season." I suppose her husband, my uncle, was dead or disappeared. Eileen liked eating at Bridie's, where meals were tasty and regular. Mrs. Killem employed a girl, an orphan with large eyes and a crazed air.

My mother trod heavily across the yard, taking her time there while I finished Maxie, tucking in his bed corners. I couldn't blame Eileen who chose to dance, I couldn't blame my mother who preferred her bed and the magazines. The spoon handle had made me sticky. I couldn't blame anyone. My father coughed, clicking away behind his newspaper, ignoring his family, ignoring his vegetable son. I remembered Sarah in the Bible, who had conceived late. It was unthinkable that my parents still did it. Maxie had not quieted tonight, restless despite his food. The priest said St. Dympna was the one to help Maxie, patroness of lunatics, I didn't believe it. He was beyond helping. I had forgotten to put the brown powder, concocted by Mr. Killem, in my father's saucer, cure for his chest. He let out a cough at the moment that Maxie spat into my face. I had forgotten his habit of retaining the last mouthful. I felt as burdened as a hospital matron, unpaid.

My mother should have married another person, or run off like her sister. I envied Bridie, whose father was the opposite of mine, pillar of the church, living and believing in his Bridie, instead of coughing behind a paper and fiddling with teeth or eyebrows. Each night when he got home my father put his cycling clips beside his cap, having stored his bike in the henhouse. He did nothing more until morning. The leaky shed was a convenient place for the bike, though hens roosted on the crossbar and saddle, whitening the pedals. He took a damp flannel out each morning, to wipe his bike. For this doleful man my mother had given her youth, her faith, the comforts of her earlier days. Her face looked radiant when she spoke of those times, how my grandparents' table was never without thick cream, dark jams in crystal jars, roasts in dark gravies, barmbrack cakes dark with fruit, all served on linen cloths. She and her sister wanted for nothing. Now it was sliced bread from a package. A torn piece of plastic covered the living-room table. Only the living room and outhouse were used now, with Maxie ruling the old parlor. Our walls were powdered with mildew. My thin Protestant mother, expecting her life to flower, had become a fat Catholic, old before her time. Her odd kind of humor remained the same, the more awful the circumstance, the funnier. When her faith changed she put holy water fonts inside doorways. The little sponges in them were hard with disuse. Fluff had collected in the metal links of our rosaries, looped over hooks along the dresser, on show for when the priest called to see Maxie.

My dress collar was wet from spat-out juice.

"Did Boyo finish, then? You gave him a wash, there's my little pet."

My mother took the cup from the table, and his flannel. She'd brought in another piece of soap, sniffing appreciatively. We would burn lavender sometimes, sprinkling the flower heads on a heated shovel, walking round his room like priestesses, to fumigate and deodorize. Lavender grew on a bush under his window. The smell would always remind me of sick people. Smells clung. Curtains, bedding, furniture, were permeated. My mother put his cup and flannel in the outhouse, returning with a newspaper, using it like a fan. Her pupils were a faded color. She could see the merry side of it. Lord God Lord, her Boyo smelled worse than a sewage plant.

"I just wish that he wouldn't spit."

She unwrapped the soap. "It's dreary for him in the bed, day and night."

"It's dreary for me and Eileen."

"Dreary? You must make of life what you can. Here is another shift, Boyo."

She settled it over his big head. Made by Miss Taylor, the shifts were the same weak gray as his eyes. Miss Taylor wasn't my mother's true friend; she pretended, in order to find out what she could about us, to pass on to the other fat women. Miss Taylor was deferred to, the first to sniff scandal. She made clothes for her friends, earning her bread. She didn't charge my mother for the shifts, stitching them free in the name of friendship. Apart from her and the priest, no adult came near us. Once Miss Taylor came at the same time as the priest, who had displeased her by his jokes with Maxie. The priest tried to engage him with shapes made from communion cloth, rabbit ears, birds, strange creatures. He was irreverent to fool with church vestments. My mother stroked the shift now, glad of Miss Taylor's kind friendliness.

"He isn't getting better. He is worse. If Eileen leaves, I'll never get to dance."

"The weather will cool down. He will improve. She went and took your turn tonight? The demon. Did she get a word yet about a position?"

"She's gone out, wearing my blouse and pink shoes. She got a letter from the gas people. In the city."

"Gas? A shop or factory? Isn't she the girl?" Laughter started in her eyes again. Her own niece working to supply homes with gas. Eileen was a gas. She'd be a

24

loss in the home, as good as one of her own children. She would send parcels. Sour jelly, hens' eggs, would liven a city diet. Either Miss Taylor or the priest might have contacts, make Eileen welcome in her new residence. Apart from the London aunt, we had no relatives anywhere.

"It's the dance. How will I get out?"

The wooden parish hall, the three-piece band, beckoned. Would Matthew be there? I wished I could tell my mother about him, have her laugh, hug me, talk about him. She touched Maxie's coarse hair. Eileen got touched by the laddos. I was deprived. Once, before Maxie was born, I remember a picnic, my mother, Eileen, and I in the orchard, laughing, trying to walk on our hands after eating bread and jelly in the orchard. We'd used dock leaves for plates and been glad. The greenhouse had stood then, with tomatoes in clusters, green ones and orange shading to deep red. There'd been more than one cockerel, the hens had been tagged, with records of egg yields. Gone now, changed, and still changing. Saturday after Saturday would go by without me at the dance. I wondered if I'd ever stop dreaming and thinking of Matthew, who'd handed me red flowers and smiled a gentle smile. His cheeks had been soft, the only male cheeks I knew, soft with a round feel.

Everyone I knew had blue eyes. Maxie's were so pale they were almost white. My mother's were a faded denim color. Eileen, after makeup, had violet-colored eyes. Matthew had said mine were the color of Wedgwood china. Sometimes I'd cry in my dreams for him, cry for a romantic life, like girls in films who ran up the steps of ancient monuments to join with their loves for eternity, or, after a few years' sorrow, reunite with a long kiss before the cage of some rare animal in a zoo. I liked films with rain, fog, snow. The parish hall didn't show films now. The fun consisted of whist, rummage sales for the fat ones, and the Saturday dance. There had been an attempt made at a dramatic group. Eileen had joined, shone, but it had broken up. For the men there was Fagin's bar.

I was glad of my weekend job with Mr. Killem. He let me have shampoo, sachets, chipped soap, cough drops, broken candles. I was afraid of Mrs. Killem, a modern mother, with hoop earrings and tight skirts, who didn't come near the shop. Mr. Killem was kind. Knowing him made me understand how tense our house was. He made prescriptions for sick animals as well as humans. Each Saturday there was a rush for his hangover mixture, a patent cure containing bicarbonate and laudanum, certain to steady the foot, cure the aching heads of the men who'd lingered too long at Fagin's the night before. The veins in their eyeballs, their puffed features and lurching, made it needless to ask. I reached for the bottles with sympathy, trying not to notice their hands. Mr. Killem relied on me on Saturdays. He bottled medicine for cows, horses, livestock of all kinds. He nodded his firm chin when I described my father's cough and mixed a brown powder. I never spoke about Maxie. He'd let me work that summer holiday, on the understanding I could stay home if I was needed. I would have worked for nothing for Mr. Killem.

The first Friday of each month was fair day, held in the next village. These Fridays were high spots. Eileen and I would wake early to listen for the sound of the slatted wagons traveling the flat road. We'd go down into Maxie's room to look across the fuchsia hedge, at the baaing, mooing, cackling creatures passing by.

Poorer farmers still drove the beasts on foot, with dogs and the help of a stout thorn stick. All day the square in the next village blared with the animals' noise. Trapped into pens, displaced from their farms, scared of the shouting farmers, they panicked. The bargaining was noisy, the men's faces reddened as the day wore on, their red hands exchanged notes, having been spat in first, for luck. A donkey once broke into our gate, as if anticipating his fate at the fair, had made for Maxie's window above the lavender bush, hooves clicking on the path. He'd stared past Eileen and me, at the bed behind, at Maxie, lying lumped, mouth open. The donkey parted his yellow teeth, pulled back his lips, letting out a bray of fearful strength. I was afraid, but Eileen opened her own pink mouth and brayed back. People in the village put up boards in the square against the rush of cattle in case they became uproarious. The howls of customers were still remembered in the co-op when a bullock broke in, to make havoc of egg crates and a stack of baked-bean tins. A dog had got gored. After the fair days, carousing lasted late. Single women locked their doors, the married waited, fearful or resigned to the one who would come stumbling in at dawn.

The bullock in the co-op had been better drama than anything put on in the parish hall. Great drafts of hangover mixture were downed in Killem's, whose shop served both villages. It was that fair where our old stock had been sold, when our farm started to go down. My mother still missed pigs. A pig was a family's best friend, eating all kinds of scraps, unlike a hen. At killing time not part of a pig was wasted, only its teeth. Affectionate, not intelligent, her pigs were a loss. My mother felt pity for those with drunken husbands, a drunk could cause a misery. My father was a Pioneer, though didn't wear the badge. My mother explained when I was young, with tears of mirth in her eyes, about the Pioneer Total Abstinence Association of the Sacred Heart. Lord God Lord, she was lucky he'd signed it, saved a lot of misery. Eileen said Maxie outdid any drunk, which my mother called demon talk.

"You'll get to the dances, Eve. I shall see to it."

She turned back the cuff over Maxie's great white hand, dodging him as he aimed a blow. Her lips twitched. Naughty Boyo.

"You promise, Mammy?"

"You'll get there. I shall see. It's quiet here, I know. Eileen will be missed from the house. You're thin-skinned, Eve, too thin-skinned."

"What do you mean?"

"If you were like Eileen, hard, life would be easier."

"I'll never leave you. Not while you want me."

"You will. You'll get a husband. Lord God Lord, there's your father."

A rustle of the paper signaled that he wanted tea, a last cup near his elbow. My mother neatly placed the pill on Maxie's tongue. Peace now for a while. She wished all the same that Eileen had more of an education, the name on the bit of paper counted in the long run.

"I'll get a teacher's post nearby, when I'm qualified. In the town perhaps. You'd like that, Mammy?"

"I would, of course. Would you ever be my pet and clear the outhouse, put away a few things before you make tea?"

"Go on back to bed, Mammy."

I didn't know how I'd manage without Eileen's company. Our home would have felt more secure with religion to practice, there was too much negligence. My mother loved her bed, caring only about Maxie. Meals were slapdash. Eileen's thieving went unchecked. We stayed out to any hour. Like my father my mother was careless about her own cleanliness, dabbing two fingers under the tap to pat at her eyes in the morning. A rinse after the hen feeding. She yawned often. Laughing and sleeping were her weaknesses. She rarely left the house. Hadn't she enough without going to others' homes, best keep to ourselves. I bought groceries from the co-op. Eileen described the Killems' meals, the meat in wine sauce, cheesecake served with cherries. Bridie learned cookery as well as French. Her parents were not troubled by Eileen influencing their daughter. They'd done the groundwork, were confident she'd not stray, find a good Catholic husband. Eileen liked their meat particularly. Bridie liked our food, enjoyed the contrast, enjoyed eating eggs at the Joynes'. Joyne eggs, fried by my mother into hard balls, exploded fat when you prodded them. Our yolks turned black with overboiling. At the Killems' the omelettes were fluffy, light as snow, flavored with delicacy. I'd never eaten a soufflé. I'd miss the sight of Eileen chewing fat off our cheap bacon while talking of Bridie's table. She was more than a cousin to me. Eileen, don't leave me. In two years I'll be a teacher. Two years is a long time alone. Stay with me.

I did the tidying, pushing things out of sight. My father didn't acknowledge his tea. My mother, stretched out in the blankets again, had nibbled some buttered toast. I was her pet to wait on her. Was Boyo in noddyland yet? Had Dadda got his tea? I heard his teeth click at the cup rim, letting the tea sip by sip through his moustache. Maxie was quiet. Now I could go out, the chores were completed, now for the hawthorn, now for the smell of the night orchard. I didn't care if hawthron was unlucky, it looked pretty in my room. I wondered if Matthew would have picked me had Eileen been there at the dance. I had no spots, my jaw was rounded, my hair soft, I had the more unselfish character. Matthew, with his training, would surely have insight into character, would know what lay behind a face, seeing so many at his work, faces screwed into grimaces of pain. He would know quality, would choose me had we both been there. Don't leave me, Eileen. City life won't suit you, stay here with the hens, the singing under the blossoms, stay here and dance.

I picked a big bunch. I went in.

I woke later to hear the outhouse door click, heard Eileen's bare feet on the stairboards, heard her cross the landing. My parents slept. Maxie slept. I heard the slip of bare soles again. I smelled lavender. I heard the click of my blouse buttons hitting the floor, the click of earrings. I could just hear her hum, a small sound, openmouthed, more of a whisper. *"Mais oui, madame. Mais oui, madame, que vous avez un beau bébé."*

"Nothing above knee level. I'll make nothing short, Eve."

"It's so old-fashioned. Please, Miss Taylor."

"Don't ask me. I will not contribute to the immodesty of this country."

"Please."

"Don't ask me. Immodesty speeds our country's ruin. So your cousin left you?"

"She did. Eileen left last week."

"Ah, I knew it. Your poor mother, after all her trouble, rearing the girl. How did she take it?"

"My mother doesn't mind. We are not obligated. Eileen wasn't."

"No gratitude. She shouldn't have left. I remember when she came, a tiny child. Where did she go?"

"I don't exactly know where."

"You don't know? Is she across on the other side?"

"She went to the city by train."

"Ah, your poor mother. If I'd my time over again, I'd still choose spinsterhood."

"Bridie went too. Eileen didn't go alone."

"I know, I know. Renegades. I'd have considered the Killems to have more sense than allow it. Eileen hasn't written?"

"Bridie wrote. I saw the letter she sent her parents."

"And Eileen didn't communicate with the aunt and uncle who reared her. Don't ask me to comment."

Bridie had written dutifully, saying where she was, with no mention of Eileen. My mother didn't worry. Eileen would land on her two feet. My father remained silent. Mr. Killem had shown me Bridie's letter, pausing from pounding his mortar to fish in his white pocket. His customers liked to see him grinding his mixtures, genuine cures compounded under their gaze. His home was modern, at work he kept to the old methods. I searched through the letter with the city postmark for a reference to Eileen. I missed her more than I'd feared. The outhouse each evening without her was a threatened place. She'd gone to her razzle-dazzle and forgotten. Sounds in the house, the gobbling, the wheezing, and my mother's giggles were worse, more uncanny. My mother spent longer upstairs, rising later, going up earlier, having rested each afternoon. Mr. Killem's assistant, Mr. Canner, was a comfort. He understood, knew how I missed Eileen. Since she left, he pushed my hand into the cough-drop jar often, knowing the solace of sucking. He sucked mints himself to conceal his whisky breath. He taught me sympathy for the Saturday regulars, having their affliction. Shared suffering brought compassion. He boosted trade. The fat women whispered. A chemist's was no place for weakness, unreliability, no matter about being kind. He watched me read Bridie's letter, understanding. Bridie was at a hostel for Protestant girls in the city. "Don't let life get you down. Just catch the clouds," he said.

"I expect Eileen is in the same hostel as Bridie. A Protestant place."

"Ah, Protestant. Don't ask me to comment. Digging

with the wrong foot, her scarcely out of her own home. The Killems won't like that."

"Mr. Killem didn't say. Please, Miss Taylor, shorter."

"Don't ask me. I will not. Protestant. A wrong turn, the worst turning."

"Bridie said it was quite nice. I'm not asking you to make me look cheap."

Miss Taylor's workroom was clouded by the dust of a lifetime of dressmaking. Above floor level, she was tidy. She couldn't bend because of her weight, couldn't touch the floor. She sat on a stool to pin my hem. Underfoot were the fashions of years back, traceable by snips of material, old pattern illustrations, buttons. Ends of swatches, dirty lace bits, beading and buckram had shifted into the corners, giving a rounded appearance to the room. It made you sneeze. She worked by electric light. Her customers had curtained privacy against pedestrian stares at all times. In spite of this, moths got in in summer, filling the glass shade that cupped the light bulb. I liked moths, especially the white kind, they died here with their wings spoiled. Mrs. Killem said the place was unhygienic, that she had been bitten. But she could afford trips to the city, expensive dress shops. The fat women relied on Miss Taylor's needle. Fagin's, Killem's, Miss Taylor's were the places of business in this village, the co-op, post office, and butcher's were in the next, where the square was. Mrs. Fagin ran a mail-order catalog business. Without Miss Taylor the fat ones would fare poorly. Miss Taylor cut seams generously, understanding the problems of her clients, their rolls of fat. She left her tailor's dummy permanently expanded under its sheet, a true friend to the fat women. She disliked bright colors

33

as she disliked immodesty. The ample fleshed went about in quiet shades, nothing flashy, as dull and quiet as armchairs.

The London aunt had sent a surprise parcel soon after Eileen went, with material inside. My mother said take it, wear it if I dared. Eileen careening in the city wouldn't bother with dress lengths, nor did we know her whereabouts. No color for an older person, purple and cherry printed weirdly, no color for anyone, take it. I anticipated Miss Taylor's wince. However, if my mother asked, she would work with it, make a dress for me. Poor Mrs. Joyne and her load of trouble. How was the boy? Was this London cotton? She might have guessed. From Eileen's own mother, was it? Ah. I coughed in the dusty air. This was the second fitting, I couldn't make her see reason about the hemline. I looked down at her cropped hair, white on her fat neck. Her head looked pin-sized on fat shoulders. She smelled of machine oil and dust. Her loose gray clothes, rimless half-glasses, Eton crop had been the same always. Oil, dust, scorched cloth left their particular smells. The glue of dress stiffening, tweed, nylon acidity, serge, old chiffon smelling of cobwebs, velvet like dry rose petals, made it a wistful place. Miss Taylor sighed as she pinned. My poor mother had a no-good sister who left a no-good niece with her, gone now, without a thank-you. Two less girls in the village, two less wanting their own way, getting it. She hadn't so much pity for the Killems. Without Eileen, the Joyne family would be less interesting. Poor Maxie was predictable, no longer exciting, a lump in his bed, making a noise. My father was always taciturn. Eileen was the bombshell, no one could match her tricks, her cheek, her face-pulling, the way she dressed. Miss Taylor would not cut cloth for Eileen, don't ask her.

"Nothing short, Eve. Why should they need to leave?"

"You can't blame them. What is there here? Not even a shop."

"What need of a shop? Haven't you the co-op not two miles away? Mrs. Fagin has her catalog mail-order business right here in this village. A home here is good enough for any girl."

"Some think it isn't."

"And the church, have you forgotten that?"

Miss Taylor took another pin from her mouth. The world could starve, erupt in volcanoes, drown in a hurricane, the church remained solid. What mattered most was who was in it and who wasn't. Miss Taylor and her friends noticed. There were few excuses. Illness, death, a person extra-drunk, birth of a child, but a mother's absence from a church was tragedy. Miss Taylor admitted that often a wife had a hard row to plow, therefore had most need of a church. My mother was courting her misfortune. Without a man of her own for protection, Miss Taylor had the heaviest shutters up on the fair days. She'd not sew for a man on principle, not even a shirt for a boy's first communion. She pronounced "husband" with a hiss of disinclination. Making Maxie's shifts was a reason to call on us, for measuring her only male client. She hissed too when she said "priest," because of his behavior. Entertaining the mad lad unsuitably, rude, scandalous dancing. She'd not heard of a girl getting a baby after twisting; it wouldn't surprise her.

"We like to think things out. Not be dictated to by an official body. Freethinkers, that's what we are."

35

"Freethinkers? What are they? You aren't born to think freely, the church does the thinking." The soul's salvation lay in duty, not in thought. That dancing furthered the rot, that and the hemlines. She dropped a few more pins, to sift down into the layers on the floor forever.

"You never saw the dance, did you, Miss Taylor?"

"Indeed and I did. Don't ask me . . . Ah . . . I saw you and your cousin. Early in summer."

I remembered her then, standing in the doorway of the outhouse, having come to measure Maxie. We had been feeding the hens. Eileen was imitating my father, wheezing, clicking her teeth, fiddling her eyebrows. Next she was Maxie, rolling her eyes, dribbling. Then we danced, our white skirts whirling over the hens' heads. We sang and flung the grain, watching it glint in the sun as the hens ran. Later my mother had said Miss Taylor must be going strange, she'd cut the shifts wrong, too small to go round Maxie, with wrong armholes, that it must be because of having no one to love, unfortunate Miss Taylor. In spite of the long acquaintance, they didn't first-name each other. Miss Taylor's cheeks were like dumplings. Flesh hung from her upper arms. Pleats of fat bulged between bust and waist.

"We were just fooling. There's no harm in a dance."

"Ah. And so the girl leaves you, without a line."

"She was to get work with the gas people. Bridie works for a solicitor."

I thought about them every day, walking the city streets to their jobs, bare-legged, toes showing through colored sandals, planning their evenings, buying more creams to paint on their faces. Would they eat lunch in cafés or save, with crisps on a park bench and some soda pop while they discussed laddos? The weather hadn't broken.

"What of your father? Did he have no say?"

"He's not . . . communicative."

"Poor Mr. Joyne."

"He didn't know. Until she'd gone."

"Ah? Didn't know?"

He'd not looked up from his salad, had continued to shred lettuce, laying slices of pink tomato and chopped egg in neat piles. His plate was more important than family comings and goings, each mouthful must be made ready. He'd cleared his throat loudly, chewed, swallowed, said nothing. My mother asked what did he think about it, would he miss Eileen? A shred of lettuce hung from a molar. He looked at her, a rare stare into her face. Why had nothing been said to him, why no word of this? My mother explained that Eileen had only left that afternoon, had taken herself off to the city, we'd soon hear where, what part she's gone to. My father choked, asked what ailed my mother, to let the girl run nowhere. Had she or had she not a job, in God's name? And what about the wages? Would she be sending anything back? My mother looked proud, she hadn't thought of that, only of Eileen's happiness. She'd not stood in her way. He said he could have got the girl into his shop, tidying, a bit of clerical work, why the big city? I knew he was thinking of her in the outhouse, he'd miss her there, as well as wanting wages. He'd said no more, returning to his plate.

"Eileen didn't discuss her plans."

"I marked her down as trouble the day I saw her on her uncle's bike. In the main street, her all of twelve, showing her flesh wantonly, wearing a bathing suit. A dirty bike. So she left without a goodbye?"

37

"She didn't warn us."

Eileen had come down with a duffel bag. Off now to the razzle-dazzle. Toodle-oo. My hand dropped the hens' wooden spoon. What now, with just that little bag? Her lips twitched. Daft girl. Demon. Where would she stay? You needed to book for the city. My mother rubbed her hairy jaw with her greasy hand. Down grew there, like a beard beginning. She paid no notice to her looks, screwing her fine hair into a bun with one pin, wearing the same dress for weeks. Eileen was a hard case, flying with her duffel bag to no address. Wait now, till she got her some eggs for the trip, something to strengthen her. Lord God, what a girl. Eileen had taken the ham bone from the shelf, and soap. My mother giggled again. She offered her journey money, which Eileen took, refusing my mother's kiss, turning away quickly. Hugs, cuddlings, were for laddos, not an aunt, no matter if she didn't clap eyes on her again. My mother blinked, touching her jaw again. She'd miss the girl and her mocking ways. We stood watching her leave. Hard Eileen wouldn't allow us to walk with her to the Killems', where Bridie was waiting, having planned to catch the noon train. Eileen left from the front door, passing the old parlor without glancing in, had turned at the fuchsia bush to look back once. She'd poked out her tongue, had broken a piece of stalk, throwing it over her shoulder in an operatic gesture. Her heels made puffs of dust behind as she trod the hot road. My mother saw my face, said not to fret, she'd land on her feet, a hard case. I picked up the fuchsia, Matthew's flower, the flower of significance when I had been kissed. He'd run the red petals down my inner arm, touched them against my face and lips, before kissing me. He'd kissed me hard, my first real kiss, leaving a blood blister on my lower lip. I'd nursed it afterward, nibbling to keep it red; a memento.

Experienced Eileen had kept a diary once, rating laddos' efforts out of a possible score of twenty. Bridie bought a diary too, to be like Eileen. Her remote looks, her superior home status, set her apart. Eileen allowed only lads with high scoring into the orchard. On hot nights I would hear them, the giggling, little gasps, the whispers. In winter not even they were worth getting cold and wet for. Now both girls were gone. Life would lose tone, color. Earlier, in the spring, they'd had a leather-dyeing craze. Carried away with themselves, they'd dyed every leather object in sight, all they could lay hands on, particularly shoes. Discussing their futures or the laddos, they splashed different colors with a special applicator, using the yard for the work. They'd made a great mess, leaving pools round the water tank. Their arms and hands got flecked, red, mauve, a particular bright blue. Excess color creased into the toes of their pointy shoes, flew up into their hair, staining the roots. They were happiest when dyeing. They didn't include me, two highly colored strangers giggling over their leather, telling me to keep off, go back to my mother. I comforted myself with thoughts of Matthew, remembering his voice. I was lovely, I was his colleen, his certain star. Just keep those clothes white till he came again. Once in the city Eileen and Bridie would change more. They would forget the village dance, laddos' kisses, shoe-dyeing. The yard was still marked with the dyes. After my one kiss my mother asked had I a cold sore, was I run down? It was after that I'd started to eat chocolate. I couldn't imagine Eileen and Bridie bearing the discipline of hostel life for long. I imagined them settling in an exotic flat, with fur rugs and house-plants, pursuing city gents.

"Poor thanks for your mother. Wanton girl."

"It wasn't Eileen's fault she was left here. She didn't choose it. Dull dump."

"Now, Eve. Don't. . . . The boy now, how is the boy?"

"He's having another bad turn."

We'd had to start tying him with bandages, the strong kind used for horses' ankles that Mr. Killem stocked. We lashed him at night. My mother went down from her bed to check him, had lost sleep. Since Eileen left, she looked more tired. She didn't laugh much.

"Poor Mrs. Joyne. Naked ways bring ruin in the wake."

"Who is naked? Who do you mean?"

"Ah. Those hems. Don't ask me. . . ."

The hula hoop too had caused her to frown. Until the twist we'd hula'd day and night, with Eileen excelling. She wanted to be an actress. Perhaps in the city her chance would come. No more meat stealing, dyeing, and face-pulling, but real acting. I thought that wanting to explore life, expand horizons, wasn't a sign of wantonness.

Miss Taylor pricked my knee. Such a color, this stuff was no color for a decent girl. Something in green, some darker shade, she could have tolerated. She kept her pins in a velvet shamrock pinned to her chest. St. Patrick had routed the snakes from our land, there was an example for you. And there was my cousin digging with the wrong foot in the city, her and that Bridie. Ruinous. Still, I liked Miss Taylor. She cared what happened to us. Also, she served orangeade with biscuits to her clients. It was cozy after a fitting to sip a sweet

40

drink while looking at her scraps on the floor. I was to tell my mother that she'd been asking for her, was sorry about her troubles. She'd be over soon to make another shift.

"It's just his fits that tire her."

Miss Taylor searched for a purple spool. She'd nothing so bright in her collection. Though pitying my mother, she managed to imply it was her fault, misfortune was retribution. I asked if she remembered Eileen's real mother. Miss Taylor said don't ask her. Like mother, like daughter. Never would she forget the sight on the bike in the street, Eileen all of twelve. She'd do the best she could with the dress. A flared skirt would be flattering. Kiss the boy for her.

My mother was bent over Maxie, trying to lift him. While I was with Miss Taylor, she'd tied him up again. His eyelids were quivering, a bad sign. I helped to haul him up on the pillows. We kept a bolster underneath his knees. She looked lined with fatigue. I told her Miss Taylor's message.

"He still has to be washed. A lick and spit will do. Is that the postman? Too early for your father."

Her hands still shook from lifting heavy Maxie. Sweat trickled into the down along her jaw. She looked older. If anything happened to her, I'd die. She took the letter from me.

"It's not that Eileen, though it's a city postmark. Demon."

"Who is it, Mammy? Quick."

She stared at me, letting the letter fall, moaning a little. "Lord God Lord, I didn't expect this."

"Let me see."

I picked up the letter, it was from the head of the Protestant hostel where Eileen was staying. The warden

41

regretted having to write. Eileen had been an undesirable influence on the establishment. Rudeness, disrespect for authority, forced her decision. She'd asked Eileen to go. She had been reluctant in view of the girl's apparent lack of real parents. Eileen had been unendurable. Her friend, under Eileen's sway, had gone too. The warden thought the aunt in the country should know what had gone on.

"Lordy lord, what a start. Poor Eileen, poor, poor child."

My mother's tired look vanished as her face twitched into a smile. Just some larky prank probably, not worth shouting over. Hard girl and her meat in the duffel bag, toodle-ooing off to nowhere. She'd like to know the details.

My mother didn't see the postcard that came with the letter. "I never forgot you, Eve. Just that I didn't find myself in your direction. Matthew."

"I didn't find myself in your direction." I read and reread the single line. What could he mean? Was our love ill-fated? What obstacles had prevented him? He had remembered me. He must have loved me, wanted and desired me, what stopped him? His direction had found him elsewhere. The words were written on the back of a picture of dark flowers, printed by an English firm. My mother went on speaking rapidly, between snorts of mirth, about Eileen and her whereabouts. I didn't listen. I had the card, holding it carefully, my hot fingers not bending it.

The heat outside was worse. Our part of the county was flat, basin-shaped, shallow, almost treeless now. The dead grass made it more bare, brown grass and dying crops. Leaves on the shrubs hung withered. The village stream was barely a trickle. No wonder the young left, it was so drab. A few of the more simple laddos stayed, the postman's son, the fatter, uglier girls. The remaining ones intermarried, so farms stayed in the same family, as ours had. You could scratch out a living from the poor soil, for real money you had to leave. Only the Killems and Fagins prospered. The Fagins never decorated. The Killems liked clean paint at work as well as home. I changed the window for Mr. Killem

43

often, to keep up his reputation for smartness. The convent ruled by Mother Perpetua, halfway between the villages, was in good condition. I liked watching the outlying children run over the fields in the early morning, with satchels that bumped their backs, containing sandwiches and pencils. That summer they'd looked like insects running across the brown fields. I had the message now, the card from Matthew, flowery and personal, a proof of his remembrance, nothing else mattered. I put it upstairs carefully, in an envelope, feeling cooler, blessed and beloved.

Bridie wrote again to her parents. She'd moved to a house in Drumcondra, again no mention of Eileen. I slept thinking about my postcard, in Matthew's pocket earlier, touched by him, near to his heart, licked by his clean Listerine-tasting tongue, his dentisty brain deciding what to write. The house got worse without Eileen. I didn't relax until my father had gone out. Now, with my card, I was consoled.

Weeks went past, no news of Eileen. My mother said she'd telephone the warden, who might know of a forwarding address, she felt responsible for the demon. Bolting was in her blood, same as her mother, who had bolted without trace for a year, returning with a bundle. She wouldn't want that again. She'd go to Miss Taylor's at lunch, use the telephone there while I was home from Killem's. My mother was exhausted. Maxie had another of his wild turns in the night, eyes whirling in his skull like blank marbles while froth flew from his mouth. All of that morning I sorted bottles between serving the Friday-nighters. No Eileen, Maxie worse, my mother at breaking point. Mr. Canner gave me a look of concerned affection. I asked Bridie's father if I could see her letter again, to make sure of no mention of Eileen. Bridie said Drumcondra was *trés gentil*, that she was well, liking her job. Mr. Killem said take a long lunch, no rush, it sometimes took time for a call to get through to the city, especially on weekends. Miss Taylor liked clients to use her telephone, an opportunity for eavesdropping. It stood in her hall by the workroom door, she listened as she sewed. A triumph, now she could hear the outcome of our sundered family, what lay behind it. Our nonattendance at Mass was well punished. Eileen, half-clad, all wantonly painted and frizzed, might well be in a fix.

My mother came back sooner than I expected, looking more herself, lips trembling into laughter. Miss Taylor's excitement had been a sight to see, Lord God Lord. She'd wanted a look at the warden's letter, fluttering it importantly, had sipped at her orange, while my mother spoke. My mother licked at her sticky lips, smiling, telling the tale. She'd got through to the warden herself. My mother imitated her English accent. Why, yes, she did remember Eileen Joyne, how could she forget her? That type of girl made her job difficult. Wrong-thinking, wild, such girls could sour an entire establishment, one bad apple spread right through the barrel. Had the girl not returned to the country? That didn't surprise the warden too much. Oh no, not considering. My mother asked for detail, considering what? Insisted she be told. The warden's voice changed, thickened, her accent coarsening. There was a limit to the vulgarity one establishment could tolerate, thanks very much. She had been tolerant, prided herself on her broad mind, but once you lost your grip, the poison spread. She'd waved aside the religious difference for the two girls from the country. She was no bigot, a heretic across the hostel doorway did no harm occasionally. She still had no quarrel with Bridie Killem, the bad apple was Eileen. That lot would make her think twice, thanks very much, about R.C.'s.

My mother pressed her further, what had happened? Unholy filth had happened, in Eileen's room. My mother's lips trembled again. "Unholiness?" What kind of "filth"? There was little harm in a bit of dust, slight disorder, Eileen was only young, what else had she done? She'd kept bad hours, late and disgraceful. Worse, said the warden. Eileen had been sick on the carpet, more than once. Lord God Lord, poor girl, drunk? The warden's voice had lowered; worst of it all, the final disgrace, was the matter of the picture. The picture of Christ himself in the hostel hall, pride of the establishment by Holman Hunt, Christ's good face had been ruined. Eileen Joyne had climbed up, changed the expression, defacing it. My mother laughed outright, recalling the story. Worse, Christ's raised hand had been extended, part of another body added. Instead of carrying a lamp, extending light over the world, a message of hopefulness, the picture had been made dark and rude. There was no place for pornography in the hostel, the warden had no choice, had given Eileen marching orders. She slammed down the receiver. My mother collapsed, squealing with laughter. Poor Eileen had knocked on the wrong door: poor Christ, the one knocking on the door, she knew the picture well, beloved by Protestants. 'Twas better than a play. That Eileen, busy with a brush or pencil, sketching, changing, had a merry heart. My mother would give her two eyes to see the warden's face when she saw the picture. English, no sense of a joke. Hard Eileen, she'd survive, that was the main thing. Tears sparkled in her eyelashes. I loved to see my mother laugh.

"Ought we to tell the sergeant?"

"Sergeant? Lord God, what for?"

"That Eileen is missing. The police should know."

She might be lying bloodied in a gutter, out of her head, or on a mortician's slab. Could you be prosecuted for picture defamation?

"She'll let us know in her own time. I don't worry."

"I could go after her. I should. I think she needs me. Will you come?"

"And leave Boyo? Have sense, Eve. You go if you want."

"I couldn't. Not alone."

"You could of course. Boyo requires me, how can I go?"

"What about . . . him? Will you tell?"

"No sense in upsetting your father at present. Eileen will land on her feet. You go." She had done as much as she was prepared to do, had telephoned. A break away from home would do me good. I must go as soon as I wished.

My teeth were still gummed with crumbs of dry scrambled eggs as I rushed off to tell Mr. Killem about going. He turned, surprised, from the funnel into which he was pouring powder. He had assumed Eileen was with Bridie in Drumcondra. He understood, was sorry that I worried. I guessed that he had not approved of Eileen, was secretly relieved that I wanted to follow her, the two alone were mischievous. Mr. Canner would do my work. Mr. Canner put his shaky hand into the cough-drop jar for me, keep at it, catch the clouds, aim mattered, not the arrival. His own aim was the bottle, but his ideas were sound. All afternoon I smiled, calm as marble, relieving sore heads with Killem's hangover mixture, packaging sweet syrup for the village coughers, ointment for sunburn, feeling better. I had a plan. I helped a fat woman with her backache. I helped a girl choose a cherry lipstick. I chewed cough drops as I smiled into the customers' faces. Illness, boredom, were like blight, attacking, spreading gloom. Only my mother seemed to like laughter for its own sake, though she laughed less without Eileen and complained that the hens were too much work. The older ones would have to go, as they laid less they'd end in the pot. I picked at the egg between my teeth, swallowing cough-drop juice. What pillow was Eileen's nightdress under? Eileen, I will find you. I am sick of eggs.

The name Drumcondra is like a water boa, known for rapacious greed. Eileen, I will hurry, before you get swallowed. I want to see Drumcondra, I want to see the city. Mother Perpetua took the upper school on a bus outing once, with food and soda pop and singing on the homeward journey. We had been bored into silence by the ancient monuments, the Dáil, the post office, once a scene of carnage, and had turned from the Book of Kells with loathing, wanting to eat our sandwiches. Now, in search of Eileen, I'd look at the city with new eyes. We'd tour together round the ancient places. I'd buy new clothes; sandals from a smart place with a bag to match. I would prune down my bust. Laddos would whistle at me, not knowing I was countrified. First stop, Drumcondra.

Mr. Killem gave me two weeks' money. Love and a kiss for Bridie. He wished I'd been the one to pal with her, not Eileen, lacking steadiness. He asked me if I'd considered pharmacy as a career. Teaching was a fine calling, pharmacy was equally valuable. Preventing ignorance or illness were both dedicated callings. It was his sorrow that Bridie never showed an interest, the secret of his hangover mixture might go with him to his grave. Already he trusted me to write labels. If Mr. Canner was a few over the top, I even mixed cough syrup, or white bismuth for griping stomachs. I handled the till at night, took in the cash. The till often stuck under Mr. Canner's hands. Rumor had it that Mr. Canner had once been a medical man, dismissed for wrong conduct. To button his smock was often beyond him on Saturdays, until he'd swigged some hangover mixture, reverting later to his own bottle. I hated to see him try to clean the sink, his pitiable hands specked like old fruit, the knuckles large and trembling. Nobody knew his age.

Of the village bachelors Mr. Canner was the most despised. His rubbery large lips, his frizz of hair, white as a nimbus round his ears, were negroid. They said he'd Negro blood from far back. No one listened to his exhortations. He was a poor exemplification of his own philosophy. On his worst days Mr. Killem preferred him out of sight. Customers needed sympathy, inquiry from an interested face, not have their bottles dropped. They wanted correct change from a till that opened smoothly, not listen to crazed murmurings from a drunk half-caste. Killem's was a meeting place, as good as any club, where you could swap symptoms, complaints, pass on the latest gossip. Cozy, nothing was expected of you, not like the parish hall, where you had to pray. Over the doorway a sign read, "Killem's purge will please. Killem's pleased to purge." I enjoyed arranging his window, keeping the glass clean, polishing, arranging the jars and bottles by their colors, grading them, straw-colored to dark. I hummed if Mr. Canner was too noisy in the back. He kept his bottle with the baby things in the stockroom. As I left he smiled, a scrap of packing straw clinging to his white hair. He gave me a last gift of candy, said remember to keep up my heart, white clouds moved above the mud. I would remember him, his kindliness, concern. He knew how I felt about Eileen.

I ironed the fuchsia dress. Miss Taylor liked frills. She'd put on a deep frilled collar. A frill was modest, a frill concealed a thick neck or thick calf, gave a flattering finish to a fat wrist. I started to press the frill. The smell of the hot purple cotton temporarily drowned the smell of buckets. I looked forward to the city, humming as I ironed. My father cracked the paper a fraction before the crash from the old parlor. I clanged the iron down as the thumps sounded, three crescendoing bangs.

"Lord God, why were you not with him?"

My mother, the cord from her dressing gown tapping the stairs behind, ran down. Her breasts showed bladder-like through the front opening. My father got up slowly, following. My mother whisked her gown shut, tying the cord before he tripped on it. She leaned over Maxie, whose eyes had turned upward, under his slitted jumping lids. He ground his teeth, the froth hung thick as a small beard from his chin, his body quivered and jerked. The noise was terrible.

"Lord God Lord, he will kill us. He's possessed."

His hand smacked out against her breast, opening her gown again.

"I'll get the spoon. His tongue, Mammy."

The force of the fit had knocked Maxie away from the wall, his bed had moved into the room, jerkingly. My mother picked up the bandages. Intended to restrain, they hung now from the bed's edge. Lord God, he'd be our end, no time for spoons, his bandages were all loose, hold him down, quick. She shrieked as he jerked again, half hanging off the bed, his bandages no more use than paper.

"Lord, help me, Abner."

I'd never heard her ask my father for anything. For the first time she could find no amusement in a crisis. This was beyond laughter. Boyo was frenetic, no time for a spoon. Help, Ab. My father stood staring at my mother's breast, unblinking, narrow-eyed, her left breast had his attention. I crouched to pull Maxie. He was too heavy. I gathered a trail of bandages. My father touched a frayed end of a torn one. Then he bent down by Maxie, down to my level. Maxie jerked less, quieting. My mother stood silent, quiet-faced. She raised up her hand, covering her breast again. Her mouth trembled. Poor Boyo had landed her a good wallop, he'd strength behind his punch, who'd have believed it? I bent again to the bandages. I felt my father's moustache touch me, his nasty dentures were close. Slowly he looked away from my mother, away from her covered breast. And now he was looking at his son. Once that son had sucked at her bladder breast. Now he was seeing him. For the first time since Maxie left the General thirteen years back, he saw what he looked like. His son lay twelve inches from his face. My father's hooked nose smelled his own son's smell. He touched the bed, picking at the bandages burst by his own son's fit. His own son had a white-foamed face, a face smeared by a massive fit. My father's ear, sprouting waxy hair, heard the creak of his own son's muscles, wrenched from inertia in the worst fit of his life. The great hand lay still, near my father's nose.

"Tie him, Abner. Do something. He'll have us killed."

My mother pulled at her gown cord again. A nice

51

time for a turn, and her just dropping off, tired by the phone call, tired from making decisions. Ab, we must do something.

Slowly my father removed his belt. The leather scratched at the loops of his trousers. The metal clicked as he tied up his own son's ankles, fastening the buckle. I felt his shame. He tied his own son tightly for his and our own protection. Our safety, the safety of our home, was risked and I felt his disgrace. Shame of the present, shame of the past, shame that he'd cut himself off, not caring, shutting himself away. Shame shut him into himself. He and his own son were alike, trapped in the limits of their own natures. He looked up at my mother, down to his son again. He pulled the strap tighter. The three of us hauled, pulling him straight, hauling his knees back over his bolster. My father's forehead was wet. My mother looked better, once he was straight. She stroked her jaw, pinching her lips as if in disbelief. We watched Maxie without speaking. Slowly his throat muscles moved, his lips opened to show his tongue, making a small gobble.

"Lord, he's alive. He's coming out of it. Boyo, my big man, I will get your pills."

"Get three, increase his dose." My father's voice was hoarse, issuing his first command regarding the care of his own son.

I looked back at Maxie. I envied him, at that moment. He'd never know pain, the true pain of the heart, or sorrow, anxiety. He didn't feel alone, he knew nothing except loneliness. He'd never face decisions. My father straightened up, went to a chair, sat down, head forward, looking at his knees. In ten minutes he had aged ten years, having seen his son, seen what his house contained. I closed my eyes. Eileen was well out of it.

I'd follow her without regret, with gladness, run after her. "Tirralombulai, tirralombulai, I'll get away, I'll get away." I felt shaky. I sat down too.

The second time took us unawares. We should have known, attacks usually recurred. This time his body hurled sideways over the edge of the bed. The leather strap snapped. Maxie was on the floor. His head came to rest against the dresser, hitting loudly, his body stretched almost from wall to dresser, a heaving carpet of gray cotton.

"Lord God, this is it. He's gone this time." My mother's hair was a loose untidy halo, wisping round her face. She spilled a trail of water. She dabbed a corner of her dressing gown on Maxie's forehead, mopping the slow blood. She dabbed with more water. My father watched her, still sitting in the corner. She said get a hanky, please, spitting on her dressing gown to remove more of the blood.

"And Ab, go to the telephone. Phone from Miss Taylor's. The doctor has to come."

"He's breathing, Mammy. Look. I think he is."

I ought to get a mirror, test it under his great nose, test it for cloudiness. His eyelids were still quiet. Eileen had taken the small mirror from the kitchen for her city face.

My father got up onto unwilling slippered feet. He'd tied up his own son, now to the telephone for a doctor to make sure the son still lived. Prematurely aged, a business failure with bad health, this was his first errand.

My mother went on dabbing, imploring her Lord God. She tried forcing the water through his tight lips. It dribbled back into the dried foam. If anything happened to Boyo, she'd have no one.

"I'm here, Mammy. You have me."

"Boyo is different. I have Abner too. Boyo is in a different class. Lord God, save my Maxie."

"And me. Ask God for me."

"Whisht now. Run for another hanky. This is all wet, pet."

When my father got back he went straight to the newspaper in the living room. He'd done all he intended, he'd resign now, resume his old ways. We dared not move Maxie. My mother and I sat on the floor, I shivered. My mother looked uncomfortable, too big for the legs under her. She went on dabbing, praying, looking wild. It was airless in the hot room. Thunder had been forecast. My bowels rumbled, I wanted to blow off, but I was in the possible presence of death. For the first time I longed to hear Maxie gobbling, his living sounds. There was only my father's paper rustling, his wheezes, my mother's quiet murmur, and my own stomach. I felt well punished for the times I'd wished Maxie dead.

He must be X-rayed. A suspected skull fracture, bruises, a minor cut, possible dislocation of his spine, a wrist sprain made hospitalization urgent. The doctor wouldn't predict, Maxie could not be judged by normal standards, no yardstick for his kind. He could revert to his previous condition, he could worsen. The doctor, impatient to get home before the storm, disliked incurable cases, lacking challenge. He'd struck Maxie from his regular rounds years back. He prodded him now, undaunted by the mess, heedless of our distress. The ambulance would take over. Had Maxie no district nurse, no regular attendant? Well, he'd be in the General for some time probably. Throughout the visit my father didn't move. He didn't reply to the doctor's "goodnight." When the front door had been dragged shut, my father lowered his paper, put up his hand to spit out a broken tooth, loosed from his dentures. He wrapped it in a corner of the newspaper. Maxie had hit hard. I thought of Eileen, how she would have liked that. Don't ever come back, Eileen, I will come.

We heard the ambulance far off, the bell loud in the hot still air, a confident loud sound in the yellow pre-thunder evening. Sound carried, sounded louder in the unnatural heat. Along the street, windows and doors opened, the people all wanted to see who was dying or dead. Whatever it was must be bad, just at the hour of the evening rosary. Ambulances were news. With Miss Taylor, the advance scout, word would be round Killem's by morning. It was a night for her to relish; first my father running to her home, no cap on his bald head, later ambulance bells. Mr. Killem might worry over the quality of his horse bandages.

Our gate clicked. We heard men's rubber boots on the path. They lifted Maxie onto their stretcher. Easy. They asked if my father would lend a hand there, the lad being an unusual weight. They didn't insist, they could manage, leave the old boy, he'd had a shock. They asked if my mother would like to come along.

"I'll come, Mammy. I'll come too. You shouldn't go alone."

"Lord God, stop smothering me, Eve. There's no need. You stay with your father."

"But you'll need me."

"Stay with your father. Maxie needs me."

Her fine hair was in strings, sweat-soaked, her cheeks shook. She had an uplifted look. Her love would save Boyo. Would I be the pet and see to the hens and tea. She would stay at the General if they would allow it. I was needed here. She could feel easy with Maxie, knowing I'd run the house. The men walked quietly with their load, my mother walked behind, her hand on Maxie's huge slipper. The men asked was he always so quiet, the poor old lad, could he talk usually? He's had a right old fall. My mother smiled, not answering. She'd changed into a clean dress, carrying her mac. I stood at the gate alone. I saw the faces, blurred and curious at various levels in their windows. Form each house more than one face peered. Curtains were pulled. The boy that few had seen was being removed after thirteen years' isolation. A bad night's work. Such a mild-looking lad, milder than milk, a saint covered with a red rug, helpless as the day he was born. A punishment for the family that didn't go to Mass, were standoffish, ex-Protestant, first-named by no one.

Inside, the house was silent. Eileen had missed it all. Missed Maxie whacking my father's tooth, missed seeing him taken headfirst through the door, one ankle bandaged, the sole bare, soft as a child. They'll plaster up his bones, they'll diagnose and prod while my mother stays there. I want my mother. I am not wanted except as housekeeper. I'll come, Eileen.

My feet made marks on the wet cement floor of the outhouse. My toes would follow Eileen's. My feet that never tanned would go after the sunburned girls. I won't stay here. I'll leave as planned. My brother, my mother, have been borne off by rubber-booted men to be healed peacefully. I can't hear his paper.

"I'll get your tea after I've put the hens in."

Inside his paper, inside himself again, locked, not needed, not wanting to be needed. He's at peace again, without Maxie. No need for guilt now, Maxie has gone away.

The hens are already inside, sensing a weather change, hidden, prepared for it. They make no sound on the perches, two are on the handlebars, one on the saddle of the bike. I must clean up the outhouse. Lift the buckets down from the sink, make room for dirty dishes. A tap has dripped, overflowing a bucket. Eileen, I will come. All this will pass, an ache in the memory. I will forget buckets, Maxie's smell, the faces peering in the evening. I will forget the outhouse, my nervousness. I won't forget the orchard, the blossoms, the fuchsia blooms and dances. I have been happy dancing. I will dance again.

I hear the privy. He's gone round again, outside in his slippered feet along the mold-green path. The latch is lifting, moving up. It's him. I'll ask him to help, the buckets, waterfilled, are heavy, a truce if not a friendship. Help me. Lord help me, don't let me show fright. He is my father, blood kin, Ab. Abner the joke in the house. Fright is unnatural. Eileen, why are you not here, laughing, thumbing your nose, sneering? Lord, don't let me believe that's his hand again. It is the hand of imagination. He's not wearing his trousers belt. Eileen. Eileen, where are you? He's whispering. The whispering is in my head. Little bugger. Knickers down. Down, down. Scrawny thighs, fleshless, crooked-looking. My face pushed back, close to his vile one. Moustache pushing, vile-smelling, pushing me. He's got me, he's gone mad. Not this. My imagination. A broken-toothed man is cutting my lip, is hurting me, a man called Abner. Not this. Eileen.

He'd gone. I lay there. Under the sink was an old Mars bar, dust-covered and forgotten. I'd planned to wash, make ready for my city trip. I would go. Leave here. There is pain here, pain and a vile taste, a smell of gray moustache. The worst is his despair. His sad, mad despair is worse than calculated wrong. He's not responsible. He doesn't understand. Worse than his own mad son who does nothing, my father perpetrated an act. He is unable to bear his own sad, mad despair.

I couldn't sleep. My skin was gritty, felt smarmed with dirt. I lay still, trying to breathe soundlessly. I sweated in uneven patches, feeling it slither either side of my eyebrows, down my backbone, inside my thighs. My bust was sore. I still wanted Eileen. Was she still laughing, singing, dancing somewhere in the city, somewhere in a place with the name of a water boa? I'm afraid, I shall be frightened for the rest of my life. I have bruises. I have pain. My head hurts. I've a bleeding lip. My back hurts. Help.

Soundless breathing, waiting for dawn. A moan of thunder, far off, less than moaning. Soon prayers will be answered. Rain. Is he in his room? Sit up. Push back the sheet. Lightning lights the room, a little blood on the sheet. Reach for my robe. I have always kept my towel, my washing things upstairs, not down with the rest amongst the paraphernalia of hens. My marble-topped washstand is a relic of the old grandparents' days, with matching china washing set. I like these utensils. Not a lot of blood, more of a spatter. Will he attack again? Eileen, he is a broken-toothed goat, I want you to help me escape. No flowers in my bowl now, no mayflowers, fuchsia, apple blossoms, just my speckled flannel. Eileen kept cosmetics, dyes, cheap

59

jewelry, in hers. What is my father doing? If I hear him, I'll run to Miss Taylor.

I don't remember getting into bed. I have been mad. A mad girl running out from the outhouse, coming to under the big tree, where the cockerel is buried, the kissing place. There was vomit. Particles of dried egg shone in the spew on the grass tips. I don't remember spewing or running out. There'd been no pain outside, but astonishment, a frightful disbelief. Now, in my bed, streaks of lightning brightening the room, I am in pain. I am not mad. It is not imagination, I am in bed, with blood, in pain, in fear. Lightning scares my mother, weather cannot be controlled, it rules nations. The hens will tremble in the shed, scared by the lit sky, birds don't like loud sounds. I must leave before worse, floods, hurricanes, tornadoes. I will rise early, walk over the far fields by the paths worn by the outlying children who run to Mother Perpetua. I'll not walk the road to get to the station. No one must see. Hurt, bleeding, I must leave unseen. Everything scares me. Cover the sheet with my blanket, leave. When the wind is right, you can hear the clock on the church tower.

My fuchsia dress looks brown in the dawn light. Still no rain, just thunder, stray flashes of lightning. No bronchitic breathing. I'm changed. The girl Matthew remembered, wearing white pleats, dancing, is being left behind. I'm off to the city in a strangely colored dress, running from someone, something. Without Maxie, none of this would be. Touching myself hurts. To insert a tampon hurts. I want to pass water. The washstand mirror shows my same face, same cheekbones, dim in the half-dark, same nose, hook-shaped. Eyes dead as dead flies under unplucked brows. Eileen tweezes hers in quirked arches, like Bridie. Under a chair is her sweater. I daren't open the chest drawer. I know which of the stairs creak, carefully carrying my case. I'll get my coat from the hook on the door.

"Eve. *Eeee-ve*."

His voice was tight-sounding, strangled, from his bedroom. He wanted me there, to go in, to bring tea. He called out for pardon, morning tea, normality. Forgive him, get weak tea. I hung on to my case. The ironing board was as I'd left it, the flat iron still on the asbestos mat, brown now from burning. I had been flattened. I could still get away, leave the messy outhouse with the dripping tap. I could still run. I would run fast, leave him. He was alone in the old farm.

"Eve. *Eeee-ve*."

His voice followed me across the yard, each syllable a plea.

"*Eeee-ve*."

I hit my toe on a rusty spike, a strut from the old greenhouse.

"*Eeee-ve*."

On past the henhouse with the planks fallen from the door inside where Biddy and the others crouched. Past the apple tree where I had been happy once, dancing, singing, being kissed. The place where the cockerel lay buried, where earlier I had vomited, the mark still there, a dried crust on the dry ground. The leaves were falling. Freak heat brings freak behavior, nature dies. I'm on the path now, going. And may God blast your soul.

"*Eeee-ve*." Faint now, far off, out of earshot. Gone.

The path was stone hard, veined with cracks under the surface dust. Get away, far away from the mad bugger. Get away from this place of inertia, where crops fail, where the land is bare. This is a barren place. The crops will die, the hens will die, the house is falling down, flee from this place. A cracked-toothed madman tried to spoil your life. Run through the dry dust covering the cracks, forget cracked mud, run to freedom. My dirty father is a cracked man. He saw his own son. He saw me. Eileen will help, will make me smile. I have no hanky. Deliver me from fright.

I waited under the thorn tree where he left his bike, waiting for the station master to open up, sitting on my case in a daze. The only one who understood how terrible home was, how I missed Eileen, how lonely I was, that I feared my father, was Mr. Canner. I needed him. Though it was still as hot, the clouds were low, dark, without sun.

"Up early, aren't you? Running off like your cousin and the Killem girl?"

The stationmaster made me jump. My toe hurt where I'd banged it, my feet were dusty from the fields. I stared at the toast crumbs caught in the fibers of his black tie. I didn't want to look higher, he had a suspicious mouth. His life was a routine one, the making of breakfast toast, the hurried shave before the day's work, punching tickets, handling cash, inquiring of travelers' intentions, as nosy in his own way as Miss Taylor. He knew where each one went, the reason. Hands that gave tickets gave him the right. He glared at my dress, bright now in the dull light, wondering why I looked strained. I could only stare anxiously at his tie. The train came. The wheels beat on the tracks "I want Eileen, Eileen, Eileen" till I fell asleep, dreaming deeply about Mr. Canner digging up the old cockerel under the tree. When he unearthed it, it had the face of a pig. The pig and Mr. Canner became one. And blossoms fell into the eye sockets and open jaw of Mr. Canner who'd turned pig, the face now turning into blossoms.

"Wake up, miss."

My nose was running. I was at the city station, hot and bewildered. Truck wheels sounded, trucks carrying mail from far places, trucks carrying crates labeled "Fragile," larger trucks with cages for pigeons, hens. There was a dog in a laundry basket. The porter who had shaken me grinned at my mortification. He'd caught me sprawling with my dress up. I had been dreaming of Mr. Canner turning pig, my pants were showing. I forgot why I had come. Where was my mother? Which station was this? Why was my toe paining me? I hit it again, getting down my case. The station was glassed in, cooler than the country one. I wanted a lavatory and a hanky. Outside the station it was as hot as ever. I remembered everything.

A woman stood on the steps leading to the street, holding a long-handled broom. She had the noticing eyes of curious people, eyes that made no attempt to conceal nosiness, worse than the fat women. What was I doing out displaying myself so early, getting noticed by porters? I had forgotten Eileen's sweater, brought with me for confidence, to make me hard. I ought to poke my tongue at the woman with the long-handled broom. I should have smashed my father's bike. I asked her the way to a cloakroom.

"A cloakroom? Just in from the country, are you?"

"I . . . I live here."

"Carrying a case? You look like a country one."

"Is there a toilet here?"

"Not this early, not here. There's cafeterias by O'Connell Street. What part are you from? Where is it you're heading?"

63

I couldn't remember the name of Eileen's street, or district. I barely knew my name. I would have swapped lives with anyone, even the broom woman. I would have liked to be her, sweeping rubbish with an everyday broom, a family at home, an interest in travelers, with little but poverty ahead. The simpler people thrived on the predicaments of others. Eileen of the unholy filth would snub her, but nothing and no one would make Eileen feel like a running sore. I worried about the bleeding.

Tea at the café with two toast rounds cost two shillings. The toilet there had no towel. Cheap blue paint crumbled from the walls in powder, dust-dry. I looked at it, touching with my finger. I had got away. The lukewarm tea had skin on it, from sour milk. I felt better after. I would walk to Drumcondra, saving my money. I passed the post office, stronghold of past troubles, with statues of Mercury, Fidelity, Hibernia. I passed big hotels and the Gate Theatre. What had engaged Mother Perpetua now interested me. I liked the thin tall houses, getting shabbier away from the city center. Smoke came from some of the cracked chimneys, despite the sultry heat. I smelled turf. Cracked stacks hung at odd angles, the smell was the same. Pedestrians talked as they walked, of weather, of storms past, of storms currently raging in the western counties, the storm prayed for in the city. Storms were the talking point, it seemed, and faces were all tanned. Mine was the only white one.

I passed the church famed for the making of novenas, extolled by Mother Perpetua. Rain had been begged for, was on its way, the radio promised it. God was good to sincere worshipers. Inside, the church was the same as all churches, the candle smell, the polished

64

pews, the incense haze, the red light flickering in oil behind the reredos denoting the reserved sacrament, always ready for the sick and dying, and many statues. I wondered if Maxie had received extreme unction, a precautionary measure. I'd do no praying. Agnostic, I'd no taste for that. I had forgotten the taste of the wafer on my tongue, melting to nothing. Like Eileen I was a mocker, mocking piety. I liked lighting candles. I'd light one under the Sacred Heart, where none burned. I would atone for Eileen's rudeness to the Holman Hunt picture in the Protestant hostel. In the dark heat of the church the face of the statue looked madder, angrier than any Sacred Heart I'd seen. Jesus, looking outraged in the gloom, made me uneasy. Was he mad or I? Might his face change? Because of what Eileen did? I'd light several, light him to an expression of more gentleness. The candles were thinner than the ones at home, the long wicks guttering lopsidedly. I used once to pray for Maxie. I couldn't pray for anyone. I'd like to forget the words "home," "family," "love." Let me find Eileen. Home is a smell of fear. A family can ruin. I pray sincerely that Mr. Canner will stop the drinking. I pray his pig's gluttony won't ruin him. I am incapable of requesting more from your mad face in which I don't believe. Don't scowl. Stop staring at me. Don't let me go mad. Love is an illusion.

I stared until my eyes watered. The beard on the face seemed to move, as though speaking. What might a statue of a man who showed his pricked red heart say to me? Eileen should not have scribbled. But for her scribbling I'd not have been ironing my dress in the outhouse at the time of the grand fit. Fate is not mapped. You make it. The beard went still as the candles guttered out, one by one, his face relapsing into

65

madness and bad temper. I looked round the stations of the cross, via dolorosa, dropping the knee at each picture as Mother Perpetua liked, venerating an unhappy journey. Against the back wall were the boxes. You prayed. You paid. The holy souls, discretionary fund, the poor, the sick, each pleading for gratuitous pennies. I plopped mine in the candle box.

Outside in the street I heard clopping. The clop of a horse pulling a cart, with pails and a tin tub on it. In outlying parts of the city men collected scraps, swill for the pigs, potato skins, calling from house to house. Rarer now, with new laws of hygiene putting them off the street, they were still to be found. Swill was a health hazard, attracting flies. Daily collection was a necessity. My mother told me of them. Like tinkers, skin men were not to be trifled with. Gypsies, tinkers, a wild lot to be steered clear of.

"Hey up, Malone. That is a gorgeous dress, madam. Care to come to Cabra with me?"

The young chap smiled, flicking his whip at his brown horse. I noticed his bony wrists and long fingers. I didn't answer. A milkman crashed bottles before the shut doors of a pub, whistling the twist tune. The city was starting the day. A cement mixer began grinding. Work on buildings progressed leisurely. Workmen busy with scaffolding stared at my dress as they clanged metal poles and clamps from off trucks. Hods containing bricks were shouldered up ladders to heights of insecurity. A claw crane swung a girder. Picks started to crack, a bore drill buzzed. Where in the world was Drumcondra? After the church it felt even hotter. Sweating dehydrated me. Dryness of the heart, emotions dried, was worse. The sky looked low enough to touch. I thought about the man on the cart who'd said madam. Madam, I'm Adam. I thought about my mother, and how much Miss Taylor knew about my unsafe home. The outlying children had been right to run past. I thought about the village children, pointing their fingers, jeering at what the home contained. The outlying ones didn't pause to find shamrocks or play games en route to Mother Perpetua. The city children were different, grinning, with time to spare, thin children mostly, jumping between gutter and pavement, soles scuffing on the curb. A group ran up some scaffolding, taunting the men, not frightened. They called at me. The skin man called goodbye, madam. Office girls were hurrying, chattering, heels tapping fashionably. I'd be like them, not Eve Joyne on the run, but citified, hurrying to an important job after I'd found Eileen. Everyone was noticing my dress. It was a beginning.

"Excuse me. Which way to Drumcondra?"

When the woman I asked turned round it was the same one, the station woman, without her long-handled broom now. She had children with her, hurrying them. She nodded, recognizingly, showing black teeth. Lost, was I? Not surprising. I, who said I lived in the city, lost already? She'd guessed all along I was a stranger. Her teeth made me think of a slogan in Mr. Killem's shop: "Cure all pain. Pain killed with 'Cure-all.' " She was a friendly mother, inhabitant of a poorer part, was going my way, join her party, I was welcome to match my legs to hers in her cracked men's shoes. I was a face to confide in, now she had finished work. Her calves were flabby, mauve-veined. Her elbows needed sewing. She wasn't alarming once we got talking.

"You'll have to step up, we're late. That station job. Fares is too dear for the likes of us."

"I'm saving too. I'm looking for my cousin in Drum-condra."

"If I were to elucidate the mileage . . . I do be tired of life. My man doesn't drink to immoderation but the money goes."

"I know. I quite like walking. I got here this morning."

"I knew it when I saw you. Walking is well enough if you've the choice. See, look at their shoes. You would need twenty pound. I do a night job, as well as the station early."

"I hope I find my cousin."

My first city friend, whose children's clothes were spotted with porridge and snot marks, made me welcome. None of their clothing buttoned, the holes were ripped. Feeling free, lighter, listening to her, I felt one of them, part of her family, running along the city street.

"I miss Dympna. She's my eldest, working for the mentals. Ward maid. She comes home of a Thursday. A light in the house, Dympna. I do be tired out."

"I miss my cousin a lot."

"There'll never be another like Dympna. The boys working the railways across over the water are no loss. It's Dympna I do miss. She helped me with this lot. See their clothes. Years more of schooling before they're off my hands."

"My mother used to rely on me. She'll miss me quite a bit."

"If I were to elucidate the trouble those boys over the water gave me. They're welcome to stay away."

"I had . . . have a brother."

"And these schoolies. That station job . . . Lookit, I do be tired out."

"Have you more at home?"

"These is the last, thanks be to God and his mother. What use is boys? A light in the house was Dympna."

The schoolies didn't look troublesome to me. Cowed, scuffing their gym shoes, they said nothing. We crossed another bridge into a still poorer area. I would like to replace Dympna, to be a light to her. I wanted to belong.

"I left my home too. I'll stay here probably."

"I knew it, guessed. At your age. Have you a feller after you? Somebody wild for you?"

"Nobody like that . . . no." Them big things. Little bugger, down. Stop remembering. Get friends. This mother is a friend.

"You wait, girl. Love can be cruel. If I were to elucidate . . . I do be tired out. My name is Mrs. Carter."

"I'm Eve. You . . . have you a hanky you could lend me? I'm without."

"My man, C. Him, had work in a slaughterhouse. We'd meat in them days. Liver and blood for black pudding. Here, take this for your nose."

"Thanks. C. Him? Why do you call him that?"

"He is my man. Carter Himself. He changed, went into the plastering. That's what marriage did, filled up the home with babies, and meat a luxury. Work, more work. Is that dress new?"

"I got it for dancing."

"Dancing? That's where I met C. Him. Dancing can make for a peck of trouble."

"My cousin and I love it. She left . . . a while back. With a school friend, Bridie."

"It's later when you wonder what it's all about. Not the wherewithal for a bus ticket, much less a few pigs' trotters for the tea. Past where that police feller is standing, that's where you want. Over there."

"You're not leaving me?"

"This is the way to the school. Goodbye now. You've a quare look of Dympna about the eyes. Stranger eyes. Are you quite well in yourself?"

"Don't leave me. Stay. Come my way, do."

"The schoolies is late already. I see them to the gate. You've no cause to worry, you are young, you're strong. Out in your figure in a gadabout dress, you'll get a feller. Them is all government housing. Girl, take care."

I watched her running with her scruffy brood. She'd given me a dirty piece of rag. There was another growl of thunder. I wanted to hear more about Dympna, about C. Him—being welcome at home before he turned to plastering. I wanted to know the names of the lads over the water, working the railways. I wanted the schoolies to like me, to have my own hair raked by Mrs. Carter's bitten nails. To be raced through streets and not afraid of thunder. She was gone now, out of sight, leaving me to walk up the garden path to a mauve doorway, the address that Bridie gave her parents. Eileen must be behind this door. I felt weak again. Aside from the toast, I'd not eaten since yesterday's egg at lunch.

The door opened as I raised my hand. There was Bridie looking at me, her mouth a surprised ring in her white face. Her hair was fringed now, a gummed-looking flap over her hooky eyebrows. The sticky hair, the painted cross expression, it was a doll's face. She had black patent shoes, a matching bag. Her skirt and tight black jersey were citified.

"What do you want?"

70

"I've come for Eileen."

Her mouth quirked. She looked exultant, a happier doll. She jerked a patent shoe, her knee moved under her tight skirt. She'd always resented me, wanting Eileen to herself. She'd learned to twist with difficulty, had envied our times with the hens, our freedom from religion, our outhouse secrets, our singing. Now I was the sorry one, she could smile into my pleading face. She knew more about Eileen than I.

"She *was* here."

"Was? Has she gone? Where, Bridie?"

"She left."

"Where to? Please, tell me."

"*Je ne sais pas*, my dear. She just went. Took off with the wind."

"What happened, Bridie?"

"I am the only boarder. We fell out, *actuellement*. I'm staying alone, if you must know."

"You must know where she went."

"*Mais non*, my dear. I don't."

Never had French syllables dropped more sweetly from sticky pink lips.

I heard another voice from the end of the passage behind her. The carpeting was mauve too, like the walls with mauve paneling finished with beading. The banisters shone cream and mauve alternately. Bridie's landlady stood in the kitchen doorway, wiping marmalade from her mouth. She wore a dark mauve coat and hat. She looked furtive, a thin nervous lady.

"Who is that you have, Bridie?"

"Just someone I knew once. No one special. *Au revoir*."

Bridie slammed the door behind her. I was surprised anyone could wear black wool in that heat. She told me to hurry if I wanted to say any more. She'd a job to go to, was late for it. She tapped along the crazy paving with her high thin heels. The path curved round a small lawn with gnomes and a few roses, brown-petaled now. Bridie patted dark red nails to her yawning mouth. The weather killed her, *absolument*.

"Does your landlady know where, Bridie?"

"All she knows is her passion for religion and marmalade. She won't help you."

"Why did Eileen go?"

"Well you may ask. She owed money to the Marma-ladey. That's what Eileen called her. To her face. She overstepped the mark. She stole from the Marmaladey's purse. She pinches things. She pinched my makeup."

Bridie's face pinched at the momery of Eileen's thieving. Her high heels stamped the pavement. I daren't ask if Eileen had scrawled more rude things over the mauve clean house. On walls, or on those fat gnomes' bellies perhaps.

"When did she leave?"

"A few days back. I can't remember. Went with the wind."

"I was relying. . . . She needs me."

"*You?* Hardly. She will survive without you, *je t'assure.*"

"I've *got* to find her."

"*Vraiment?* She's just a cousin, isn't she? Not a lost love."

"There's been . . . trouble. Trouble at home."

"There is my bus. '*Voir.*"

"Wait, Bridie. Please wait."

"That picture business. A Prot hostel, granted. She went too far. She owes me cash too. '*Voir.*"

Bridie smelled of faint violet as she moved. A bus

drew up. A car hooted, the driver craned at her. She'd no need of Eileen now. No need of anyone to imitate. She had her own identity. That round mouth in the powdery face, that tilted nose, those heels needed no guide, they had their own direction. Bridie with her knowledge of French would get the life she sought. She jumped on the bus, catching the chrome rail with her dark nails, not looking back. Her head was full of her new job, her new life in her new black clothes. Goodbye, Bridie.

I walked again, along the same street, sadly. I might see Mrs. Carter, the city mother, coming back from the school, without her schoolies, who would have more time for me and my problems. I'd listen to any advice, the sight of her rotted teeth would be tonic, I would enjoy hurrying with her, beside her cracked men's shoes. But there were only strangers. You rarely saw the face you longed for, especially in crowds. Fumes from the traffic were especially strong in the oppressive heat.

The black Liffey water reflected the heavy sky, blacker, more uninviting than tar. The surface reflected floating corks, straw fragments, tobacco packs, thrown carelessly. A swan swam at a crust. People lingered on the bridge, a place of watching, of taking stock before you crossed to the richer side of the city. Such a black sky was uncanny. Sad, black as the Styx, the river didn't please me. I would go to the gas showrooms. They would know about Eileen, would give me her address. I might find her sitting there, with letters in her hand, bent over a desk dealing with the problems of city dwellers, wanting gas. I needen't look further. I'd fiind her making her colleagues laugh, imitating them, my Eileen. I had achieved nothing by charging to the

73

north side, except that I'd met Mrs. Carter and discovered that Bridie disliked me. Eileen's square-jawed, sneering face would be waiting for me.

The supervisor was sweating more than I was. An impatient woman in a murky office, she had little time to spare for relatives of the staff, particularly absent staff. My cousin had left without a word, had failed to appear one morning. No, she knew nothing. To be frank, she found it hard to have sympathy with such girls. Up from the country, with little or no ambition, Eileen had not wanted a career in gas supply, had used the office as a launching point before traveling on. Presumably she'd gone to the other side, like so many others. Emigration was Ireland's curse. A cheery enough girl, who had not stayed long enough to earn a reference. The supervisor glanced at her blotter. She was a busy woman. She fanned her face with a form, not looking up again.

The storm broke as I came out. Gigantic thunderclaps, with forked lightning filling the black sky. Then rain. The longed-for, prayed-for rain pelted onto the pavements, smashed onto shop awnings, gurgled down the gutters. The force of the rain hurt the skin, little hammer blows. People cried out, lifting their hot faces quickly, then running for cover. Because it was too sudden, this was too much, unexpectedly painful, wet. They ran in all directions, anywhere, to any door for shelter. I ran too, my feet slipping in my sandals. My toe hurt me again. My dress dragged, a pull like wet skin, impeding me. There was a stink of drains.

"Watch it. Watch where you are going. Mind there."

I felt the rope round my waist. I didn't see until too late that the manhole had been left open.

"Lord God Lord, what got into you, Eve? It was God's broad daylight."

"The storm. I couldn't help it, Mammy. Who told you?"

"The hospital got in touch with Bridie. The address was in your bag. Bridie telephoned Miss Taylor."

"It was the weather. I couldn't see anything. I didn't know there was a drain."

My throat ached. I felt I'd swallowed stones. I hated to think of Miss Taylor's delight at having to lumber over the road to tell my mother about me falling into some kind of a cesspool in the big city. Poor Mrs. Joyne, first the sick lad falling from his bed, then the daughter falling in a hole. More bad news from a hospital, a city one this time.

Rain dripped from my mother's earlobes, along her furry jaw, oozed along her coat hem, dribbed down her bag straps. Her hair hung in strings. She didn't kiss me. I guessed she hadn't wanted to make the trip. I was a nuisance, falling down drains instead of heading for shelter like decent folk. She'd had to take the train in this weather, alarmed, put out, only to find me well. I smelled fearful, though.

"Gas pipes, so they said. They were laying pipes. Why didn't you take care?"

"I couldn't help it."

"Not that they had any business leaving the hole open, storm or no storm. No sense to it."

Her mouth began to tremble, her eyes were already shining with mirth. It had its comic side.

"Don't, Mammy."

"But a hole. Lord God, it's so unnecessary. Didn't you see the rope?"

The nursing sister had been terse. This was a casualty ward, not for minor mishaps. This was for grave accidents, emergencies. I was a hysteric, wait for your mother. There was nothing wrong, I was a lucky girl. Not all had a loving mother. Now she was here, her bag straps soggy, gloves in her hand, not looking loving, she was laughing.

"I'd been to find Eileen. I can't find her. She's left Drumcondra. She's left her job. You told me to go after her. I can't help it if they leave manholes wide open."

I still felt sick, sick from the wet slime, the jangling, jarring, sick from humiliation. The men who'd neglected their work, had left it unguarded, had run back to me, had pulled me by the armpits, appalled. The prayed-for rain had caught them out. They got me a taxi. They delivered me to the nurses. I was cleaned with warm water, given an aspirin, but no sympathy. A mercy I'd no bones broken. Stop that fuss, go to sleep. When I slept I dreamed of a pool of manure, of drowning while Mr. Canner blessed me with a freckled hand. It was then the sister got impatient. I was to stop shouting in my sleep, I was a lucky girl, they'd telephoned, my mother was on her way. Just sleep quietly.

"You were ever clumsy. But roadworks, Lord God Lord."

"I am not clumsy. I am neat. I'm hurt. I hurt everywhere."

How could she dismiss my agility? Hadn't I been the first to twist? Hadn't I used the hula hoop before Eileen or Bridie?

"I have spoken with Sister. I told her you were having a little break. You need a holiday. You can leave the hospital in the morning."

"Where to? I've not found Eileen."

"I know. Eileen is all right."

"Where is she?"

Nobody cared about Eileen but me. My mother spoke offhandedly, glancing at her gloved wrist, pulling at the wet material.

"She is the other side. She went to London."

"Where?"

"She sent a card. No address. Perhaps to her real mother."

"You didn't tell me."

"I've not had the chance yet. Lord God, the sight of you."

"Aren't you concerned about her?"

"I am of course. I raised her like one of my own. My only sister's child. Eileen is all right."

"I need her. I came for her. I must find her."

"Stop worrying, pet. Stay here in the city. I must be getting back."

"Don't go. Don't. Where shall I go? Is Maxie better?"

"He's grand. Gone quiet in himself. He's not the lad he was, not since the fit. They're keeping him."

"For good? He won't be coming home?"

"Lord God, there's no saying. We don't know yet."

She wasn't upset. I'd never seen her eyes so happy. The lank wisps round her forehead started to dry prettily, making a frame for her face. She fished in her bag for Eileen's card.

"You'll be alone at home. Without the three of us, what will you do?"

"Alone? Do? I have Abner."

Her face and voice shocked me. She said his name lingeringly, with delight. She cared nothing about my plight, my lostness, she only wanted Ab. She'd changed overnight from a martyr with a sorry life into a doting wife. She wiped her nose. To speak his name gave her a melting expression, like a woman on her honeymoon with a bright new ring instead of the wire-thin one left her by my grandmother. Her real wedding ring had fallen into the hens' bucket years ago. Perhaps my father would get another for her, now she was young again.

"Don't you miss any of us?"

"Ah, pet. It's rest that Ab and I need. Rest, alone on our own. You stay here, stay in Drumcondra where Eileen stayed."

"I can't. They . . . Bridie doesn't want me. You don't want me. You're always resting. In bed. And him with his newspaper."

"Whisht. A holiday, pet. A break and a holiday."

"Why?"

She didn't answer me. Her voice changed, softer, her face pinking at the memory as she spoke of the walk she'd taken with Abner, before the rain came, alone in the far field. She dabbed at her eyelids, overcome. She wasn't interested in the new pale Bridie, who had got Frenchier, or the landlady with marmalade on her lip, or anyone but herself and Ab. They'd walked, hands held, treading the parched ground of the far field. She said don't fret about Eileen, she was grand, would always land on her feet, that one, the demon. She didn't care at all, we were all off her hands. She knew our geographical location, could forget us. Eileen had been caught stealing, had drawn scatological graffiti. I was in trouble. Maxie might never return. Forget it all.

"Mammy."

"What, pet?" She flicked another look at her watch. "How is Biddy?"

"Biddy? Ah, the hen. Not so well. The rest of them is grand, all laying. She doesn't eat. Ab helped me with the feed this morning, and egg gathering, before he went off."

"She must eat or she'll die."

"When does your term start, pet?"

"In three weeks, you know that. Don't you want me home?"

I wished that she'd weep and beg for me, but she only repeated that I must have a change after my shake-up. She'd brought me some brown eggs. She'd get some clothes to me. In her confused new state she'd forgotten everything but the eggs.

At the door she turned to look back, said wasn't the weather a demon. Changed weather had changed her life.

I'd had no chance to tell her about being drenched and half blinded, how I had waited for them, waiting for the hands to rescue me, my hands round a metal ladder, one foot wedged in sludge, how the gutter smell sickened me. I'd heard them shouting, hurrying. I felt hands under my armpits. I'd lost a sandal. The driver of the taxi had been wary, not wanting his seat soaked. A man put a coat round me, oily-smelling, rough against my wet face, while talking to his mate. Such weather wasn't ordinary. They'd tipped the driver lavishly, from guilt. They'd asked was I in pain, worrying about their negligence, about being sacked perhaps. They hadn't made sure, had run blindly without covering the hole. My foot made the driver stare. I looked a fright. In the ward the sister asked if I always bled so heavily each month. Where were my relatives? Impatiently she told a nurse to wash my bruised parts, dab my foot with some lotion. She'd no liking for those lacking control.

Brown eggs were my mother's remedy, eggs and advice to stay. The bedding was damp, with a warm feel like used blotting paper. I pulled up my knees. I wanted to stay in that damp bed till the day of my funeral. A nurse asked if I'd like one of my brown eggs boiled, a light boiled egg would make me chirpier. Boiled was better than fried or scrambled, less bother. I could get up then. A pity about the lost shoe. The staff were all talking about the storm, settled now to a steady deluge. Lights were lit early. Crops might be saved yet. Dust would be gone, windows cleaned. Salvation was in rain. When the nurse came with the brown egg she asked why wasn't I up, to stop staring. Forget about tumbling in a hole, falling and screeching, forget mud, look on the brighter side. I had a kindly mother.

My mother would be watching the rain from the train window on her way back to the country and Ab. Her watch under her wet glove had been her engagement present, retrieved from the dresser drawer where it had lain for years, among broken knives and ends of string. She collected meat skewers in a rubber band. The watch had glistened, keeping time for her glistening new life, two lovebirds needing rest.

"Come, Miss Ingratitude, eat up your egg. What have you got to complain of?" A holiday was something most people worked hard for, especially nurses. A casualty bed was for those hurt badly, not a hotel. I'd nothing wrong. A bad period, a lost shoe, a bruise or two. I had a good country home with a concerned mother in it. Shame.

Next morning early, my father came. He brought my clothes. The sight of him walking into the ward was worse than the fall. His nose, his sorry eyes, the roots of his moustache showed over the top of a large cardboard box. He put the box down. Of tough cardboard, it was the kind used to crate televisions. Glumly he avoided looking at me. I was silent. He put the box on the end of the bed. There were holes punched in it. I saw it shake a little, then a white feather poked through a hole.

"It's my hen. Why have you brought Biddy?"

"She told me."

"I can't have her. How can I?"

"I'm doing as she said. Take your clothes and the bird."

"But why?"

I hated him for touching her, for putting her in a television box, for coming near my bed. From him I had run, now he stood watching me, crushed and dispirited with no home for myself or Biddy. A noisy bird, a hen to fend for, was too much. I hated his moustache, waxed stiff for the trip, I hated his broken tooth. Happiness had changed my mother, he was the same.

"I brought money. From me. My contribution."

He looked worse as he pulled notes from his pocket, buying mercy. Cash wouldn't buy or make me respect him. He stood staring at the notes on the bedcover, chewing his lip, the gap in his upper jaw coming and going. I leaned over to Biddy. She'd missed me to the point of starvation. I tried to feel the feathers shifting at the hole. Get out, mad bugger, what will the nurses think?

"I don't want the money." Blast your soul.

"You'll not think unkindly of your old . . . Da?" Say nothing, stay mute, cold.

"She said to. And more eggs, in with your clothes."

"She needn't. I'll not be coming back. I don't want money."

He said no more. I felt his relief that I was not returning, relief that I'd not earn more than him when I was a teacher, relief that he could pick up his money from the bed. He could live at peace now.

I watched him leave, half scuttling, anxious, not looking at me once. And now I am alone. The nurses need the bed.

The box was rain-sogged. I went on pushing my fingers in, trying to feel feathers, but she'd moved. I could dress now, I had shoes, clothes that I needed. I hoped she'd packed hankies. The sister had said that a loving family was a gift greater than rain. A loving family influenced your life journey. No one saw me leave, or helped with the television box. Outside in the rain I found a taxi. The driver was kind-faced, cracking a joke about was it a vet's or a hospital I was leaving, what animal had I there? I pushed a pound at him without looking at the meter when we drew up to the mauve door in Drumcondra. It looked darker in the wet, the crazy paving shone. It was a sanctuary of a sort. Rain dripped down the bellies of the gnomes under the rose-bushes, slithering into their crafty plaster eye-holes. Bridie was in.

"Merde. You again. Your mother fixed it for you. You're to have Eileen's room. What have you in the box?"

She didn't wait, walking ahead upstairs, not helping me. I still limped a little. She paused to pat her silvery bangs, then turned to examine a mark on her thin heel. Watch out, don't let that wet stuff near her.

"Where is the landlady, Bridie?"

"The Marmaladey? At her sodality meeting, poor old animal, gone on her religion. But for that she mightn't have taken you in, not after Eileen."

My mother's money and the Marmaladey's religion had bought me a refuge. I owed them my bed. There was an odd smell in the house, stale. Bridie said true, the Marmaladey couldn't stand fresh air, her windows were stuck tight with mauve paint. Not that she cared, she was never in long enough to notice. In and out with the wind. She hoped I wouldn't expect to be looked after, she had her own life now, she wanted no passengers tagging behind, she'd said goodbye to the country and all those there. She'd set her cap for her boss's son. No lame ducks for her. Her eyes narrowed when she spoke of Damian, son of her boss, her city laddo. She had the look of a scheming cat. She hoped I wouldn't touch her things, or she'd have to lock her door. Was there something wrong with my feet?

"I don't take things, nor do I need your help. Why should I want anything of yours?"

"How should I know? You're Eileen's cousin. Blood tells. I felt a fool, telephoning that Miss Taylor. *Merde.* Trust you to fall in a hole."

She didn't look at the box again, pausing on the landing to look into a mirror. She opened another mauve door. This was the room, the bathroom over there. The Marmaladey slept downstairs. She'd see me, probably, at tea. *'Voir*. She didn't think my dress was very chic. She shut the bathroom door to repaint her face for her evening date.

The room was cold, a potted coldness that you felt inside. This was where Eileen had stayed, her head lay on that pillow, her clothes had dangled from those wire hangers. I sniffed for any smell of lavender, but got only the thick damp smell. I touched a cold wall. Eileen had touched there as she left the room. I looked into the mirror where Eileen had frizzed her hair, singing perhaps, or practicing a dance step before going out for an evening of dancing and kissing. There was no hint. I looked on the carpet, beneath the mirror, hoping for some little trace of filth, a frizzy hair, spilled powder, an envelope corner, a torn wisp of Kleenex. Eileen of the unholy filth, where are you? A corner of the bedspread had a faint stain, paled from laundering, paler than Eileen's lipstick, odorless. There was new soap in the basin. Only my own face was familiar, looking back, uncertain, afraid.

I put the cardboard box under the bed, pulling the quilt down to hide it. I must be cunning, make a plan for the concealment of my hen. I must stay calm, think something out. I would try to train Biddy to turn her nights into days, to make hiding easier. I would leave my light on all night, drawing the curtains in the daytime. She could run round at night, wearing her legs out on the mauve carpet. With stealth and planning I could keep her in my room. I would put newspaper down, not to be filthy like Eileen. This would be Biddy's orchard, till I got someplace better. The box under the bed would have to be the nest. I'd make her eat.

There was no time to unpack. Bridie said if you were

84

not punctual you got no food. At tea there were eggs in a pastry pie, which we ate in a small room off the kitchenette. There was a hatchway through which the Marmaladey poked the food, closing it with a bang, leaving Bridie and me alone. The Marmaladey hadn't spoken to me yet, leaving a key by my plate. She had her room beyond the kitchen. A notice was on the wall near me. "Rules for guests. Ladies are requested to be in by 10:30 P.M. and to make no sound. Ladies are asked to be punctual at table. No visitors or pets." After the pie and hatch-closing she went out, wearing her dark mauve outfit. Benediction, Bridie said, dabbing her lipstick in a bored way. Damian was waiting. She'd see me at breakfast, *possiblement*. The Marmaladey was rather deaf, just the same, take care. Last one in locked up. I went upstairs again. I arranged my clothes. My things looked few and shabby.

"Come, Biddy. Out of there."

I lifted the quilt. I opened the box, holding a saucer of milk. She stayed back, hiding behind tufts of packing straw mixed with soiled grain. Her feathers pushed out through the back holes. I crawled further under. Her head was drooping, her beak touched her shabby breast. She looked half dead or fainting. I had been selfish to leave her so long, putting my hunger first, but now I had pastry crumbs and bread. Her neck feathers felt hot. I got some water. I started humming. Music would soothe her. If she remembered the apple trees, the singing and the sun, she might regain strength. I put my hand into the box, singing into her ill face. She raised her beak slowly, straightening her legs. She walked out, her yellow feet making a light sound.

"Look, Biddy. You have to become nocturnal. As from now. Take this."

85

I went on humming and she sipped a little. Her box was terrible. I relined it with paper scraps, taking the old down to the neat bin at the back of the house. Nothing was out of place. My mauve room was small, but the sparse furnishings would allow her space. She looked round it haughtily, one foot lifted. I settled her tail feathers. Her comb had a limp, unhealthy look, lacking pink freshness. Always small, her bones almost showed through her feathers now. I picked her up, cradling her. I took her to the mirror.

"Look, Biddy, at this moment we're alone. It's us against the world. Don't die."

It was like holding a feathered baby. We were both weary, displaced, worried, and would be dead one day. Meanwhile I would fight.

I put my cardigan along the door, so no light would show. I didn't know the time. I removed the mauve lampshade to make the light stronger. I sat on the bed after I'd washed my cold cheeks. I heard the Marmaladey's door shut after her Benediction. Last one in locked the door. Bridie and Damian were out kissing somewhere, in a car or the back row of the cinema. My mother had her Abner. Eileen would have landed on her feet, somewhere in London. I had a temporary refuge, sitting on a mauve bed in Drumcondra, listening to cars swish past in the rain, too tired to make Biddy exercise. She'd sunk into a heap where I had put her down.

When I woke up it was not yet dawn. I was stiff, with a pain in my ankle. Biddy had hopped up on the quilt, was nesting in the pillow, pink eyes tightly closed. My plan had not succeeded, the bright light did not keep her awake. She slept as if she'd been hypnotized. I had to push and pummel her against the wall to make room for my head. I got between the sheets, damp like the hospital ones. Since the deluge, nothing felt dry. I left on the light to make the place less strange. From the pillow came a faint touch of warmth where Biddy had been resting. The city was frightening.

In the morning Biddy's musty feathers were pressed close to my left cheek, almost suffocating me. I hugged her, I resolved that morning to become my own best friend, not to depend on anyone. I put her in the box again, settling the quilt neatly. Animals' and birds' habits were probably as hard to change as people's. She was diurnal.

At breakfast Bridie was crosser than ever.

"*Merci*. Nothing. No food."

"Are you ill, Bridie?"

"Gin has given me a splitter."

"I didn't know you drank."

She gave a languid pout. She made a headache sound like a sophisticated city condition. She sipped her tea with unpainted morning lips. I was used to seeing country hangovers in Killem's, serving the hangover mixture. Bridie's city one was dainty, a sighing condition that made her contemptuous, too grumpy to acknowledge me.

"I'm going after a job today, Bridie. I found out about Eileen, Bridie. She is gone. Bridie, Eileen is in London. I'm going to stay here."

"*Vraiment?* Here? *Here?*"

"Yes. I'm leaving college. I couldn't stand teaching children, I . . . I hate children. Do you like them, Bridie?"

She shrugged. She could be shrewish in her way. Damian, if he took her on, would have a lot to handle. I knew that she wanted me gone, to be the Marmaladey's sole boarder again, to be waited on as her parents had waited on her. She didn't want to pass the butter, or talk at meals. At home she'd been a prodigious eater, now she was a gin-and-bitters girl, clutching at her bangs in a dramatic way. Before she left the table she sneaked a bit of toast into her bag.

I would rather have stayed with Biddy upstairs than face the city again. I would rather stay in bed, pick at my toes, brooding over the unkind people in my life. I put a clean dress on. I would try first at Eileen's office, where I'd fallen, an address I could find without trouble.

The personnel manager frowned as she flipped through a card index.

"I'll take anything you have. I am definitely staying in the city."

"Miss . . . Miss Joyne, did you say? From the country. We have no vacancies, nothing."

"Please. Anything at all."

"I told you, Miss Joyne, we have nothing."

"I would be most obliged. I'm a hard worker. I'm not fussy. I intend to stay. I'm prepared to work up from the bottom."

"There might be something in the domestics. Night work. Yes, I can offer something in cleaning, if that interests you."

"I told you. Anything."

"It is rough work. A girl to assist our regular. But the work is hard, nor is the pay great. It might . . ."

"Please, I'll take it."

I was to start the next day. The job fitted with my scheme of keeping Biddy. I could stay with her while Bridie and the Marmaladey were out. My mother had paid a month's rent for me. By that time I'd have saved for someplace better. I'd not mind cleaning. I'd keep the showrooms shining. Mrs. Carter, the first city person to befriend me, had gripped a long-handled broom—a sign. I too would wear a coverall and have a place in the life of the city. Night work would suit me, I would become nocturnal. I might give Biddy the whole run of the house when it was empty, teach her to climb stairs. I might get weekend work too, in a bar or cinema.

"I've got something, Bridie. I've got myself work."

"*Vraiment?* Damian and I are going dancing."

"Dancing? Are you?"

"You can come if you want. I don't care."

"Will Damian mind?"

"How should I know? Come if you want. Just don't mention Eileen. Don't mention anything about home, especially your brother. And don't mention falling."

"Do you mind my breathing the air about you, Bridie?"

"*Mais non.* But do it quietly."

The Marmaladey still hadn't spoken, poking an omelette through the hatch, shutting it to eat in solitude. Bridie bolted the bathroom door, emerging an hour later, violet-scented, dressed in a sequined sheath dress with a sequined bag. City girls were never without handbags. To see her, no one would dream she'd anything to do with country times, or that a hen dwelled in the room next to hers. She repeated her orders. Nothing about the country. The twist wasn't in fashion now, forget that, forget about shoe-dyeing, chickens, convents. Stay quiet.

Damian drove fast and recklessly. I sat in the back enjoying it, cars as well as taxis were still a novelty for me. Bridie put a cigarette in a long holder and kicked her shoes off, curling her legs under her, murmuring into Damian's ear. "I've brought her along. She has nobody," was all she said of me. I didn't care. I had a job. I was going dancing. I would get used to the life. Bridie knew the coat attendant, smiling her shiny lips insincerely.

"How are we tonight? *C'est bien*?"

False Bridie. Bridie of contempt and disloyalty, floating toward Damian, mouth pursed in kissy affectation, speaking poshly. She'd told Damian she was half French, came from a medical background, her father had his own practice.

There was a flash band, the six players in their red suits darkening and lightening in the flashing crystal lights. Bridie glided. Nothing could stop her, she'd get the best available, of husbands, homes, prospects. She was disparaging about my fuchsia dress. Damian had hair slicked like a wet pelt to his scalp, and knowing eyes. Bridie said when he looked at her she lost her will. I didn't believe her. I saw their future. She'd get a home like the college girls' shrines, with material comforts a necessity. Her children would grow up thinking their country grandparents quaint, a quaint oldfashioned chemist somewhere in the wilds. Visiting would be discouraged. She'd work for her husband, entertaining formally. Her children would go to finishing schools. The giggling in our yard, the shoe-dyeing, the secrets shared with Eileen, would be forgotten.

The lights started to change color, flashing from red to mauve, to violet, to cobalt blue. The dancers grinned like gargoyles at each other. Bridie's teeth looked devilish as the lights whirled and the music quickened. I smoothed my dress. I didn't mind standing alone. I was my own best friend now.

"Excuse me. I'd know that color anywhere. That dress is gorgeous. Remember?"

"You were outside the church of the novenas. You asked me to Cabra. You had a cart and horse."

This was a city of coincidences. It was the first man who had spoken to me, the skin man, calling me madam, asking me onto the dance floor while the lights whirled. He was dressed neatly now, dancing with simple quiet steps till the lights and the music slowed. Then he led me off the floor.

"Let's talk. I think we have much in common."

It felt natural, right, to stay with him. We drank coffee and I forgot time, forgot Bridie and Damian, the dancers and the lights. I didn't have to feel afraid of the city anymore.

"**D**id you stay all evening with your corner boy? Damian and I went on to the Bailley."

"He is not a corner boy, Bridie."

"He looked it to me. *Quel âge a-t'il?*"

"He didn't say his age."

I couldn't think of him in terms of young or old, his face was outside time, ageless. His eyes had not left mine as we talked. We'd not exchanged names. I called him Skin. All that I said, my likes, my dislikes, fascinated him.

"What does he do?"

"He . . . sells things. He buys and sells. Bridie, are you going to take Damian to see your parents?"

"I told you not to mention home. Damian has a respected position."

"My chap is good. I like him."

Bridie had a new habit of pressing the tip of her tongue between her teeth after a remark, adding force to her cattiness.

"What does he sell? What did you call him? 'Sin'?"

"Skin. A nickname. He sells . . . provisions. He's nice to talk to, a good listener."

"Whatever he sells, get some of it, *ma chère.*"

Bridie's hair was still stiff as straw from the lacquer

sprayed the night before. She had a chiffon scarf round it, ready for making up after breakfast. Again she refused any food, shuddering. She'd not expected anyone to dance with me. She was annoyed that I'd forgotten, gone home without her and Damian. I still retained the glow from my evening, remembering his eyes, the corners creasing when he laughed. I didn't want to talk about him. She denigrated everything, she was worse than Eileen with whom I'd once been close. She lacked any nostalgic feeling for me. She put her cup down. Again she took some toast, buttering it with quick secretive hands, adding a little bacon and a touch of mustard, wrapping it in her mauve napkin for later. At home only the fat women had handbags. Bridie was never without hers, wedging it between herself and her chairback at meals, the lining marked with nail polish of various shades. Skin was my secret.

"What time did you get in, Bridie?"

"How should I know? I hope your hobgoblin didn't come inside. Don't spoil things, now you're here."

The Marmaladey's face appeared at the raised hatch, checking. She liked us to eat quickly. Bridie said she worked in a hardware department, that she'd no friends and was part deaf. I imagined her selling sink equipment, mops, polishes, pans, a look of martyrdom on her face. Her clean mauve home and her faith kept her going. I had been afraid of coming in late. Skin had wanted to stop at the cafeteria where I'd eaten the toast; I'd been too worried. We had leaned on the parapet of the bridge, looking into the dark water, different now with rain falling, making a fresh smell. I told him I had come after my cousin. He said I was the one who needed looking after, what with my fall. A poor introduction to the city.

He asked about home, were my parents not concerned? I turned my face to the dark water, said I'd not had much to do with them for a while. I spoke about Mr. Canner, who would be missing me. Skin looked sad, had watched me without speaking as I told him that I'd left to forget my childhood. Then he had turned to the black water, pointing at a gull flicking its wide wings in the lights from the bridge. We listened to the wingbeats. Lights and the city noises didn't disturb river birds, they were adaptable. They relished the damp air after the earlier heat. The river was high now. The gulls cried with a mournful sound. He studied birds, he told me. He loved gulls, the black-headed, the common, the lesser-backed, the little gull. He spoke of the legend of the gull born without legs, unable to land anywhere until tasks had been carried out, tests of endurance. I'd never seen a gull. I'd never seen a large expanse of water.

The rain had moderated temporarily to a mistiness. Everything dripped, gutters were clogged full, lights appeared haloed with mist. We stood, shy and friendly, observing things. Pools in the road splashed outward as the traffic wheels rolled through. Petrol splashes here and there gave a prismatic sheen. His knowledge of birds impressed me. He liked night birds too, the nightjar, owls, nightingales, he'd like to show me quieter parts, where birds could be seen and heard. Phoenix Park was at its best in autumn. Nature and wildlife, especially birds, absorbed him more than religion. He'd not a lot of time for church worship, though there were interesting ones here. St. Michan's Church was particularly fascinating with its underground vaults containing bodies centuries old, but decomposed, owing to the special dryness of the soil. Did I like rowan trees? And the silver birch and holly? Legendary trees. He never tired of nature study, we were in nature's hands. It was a mercy the heat spell had broken, though nature was overdoing the remedy, we'd have flooding next. He liked dancing, was teaching himself, that's why he'd been at the dance—to watch. He practiced steps afterward alone. I told him how Eileen and I danced.

His smile charmed me, quick, lighting his face, his eyes slitting into wrinkles, before becoming serious. I wanted to know him quickly, learn everything, yet we were already tuned, like part of each other. His wet hair curled over his ears, which were curiously shaped with slightly pointed rims. He had an ambition to travel. Clients on his work rounds gave him tea, and sometimes slices of apple cake, telling him of far countries where relatives had settled, showing him photographs. He longed to go himself, see if the reality was as good. The flora and fauna of other lands beckoned him. He was not ashamed of the way he earned his livelihood, organic matter should be recycled, nothing should be wasted, his work helped the country to prosper; important work. The farmers needed him. It pleased him to be liked, that kitchens welcomed him. He read the letters from the cousins, sisters, children, yearned to follow. He practiced his dancing steps, studied, dreaming dreams of central Australia and the Asian steppes.

He was disappointed that I had no hobbies. What was I doing in a cleaning job when I'd a teaching course half in my head? I told him then about Maxie, how he'd made home difficult. He'd nodded. He'd come across much sickness, a hopeless case could drain a family. Here in the city I could enroll in classes. I told him about Drumcondra, how my cousin had stayed there with her friend. The friend didn't want me. I asked if he knew anything about hens. I told him I had Biddy. He'd gripped my hand. A hen? He liked them, knew all about them. He'd bring her food. What was my telephone number? The bird would be a link, he wanted us to meet regularly.

"Bridie, why look down on someone for the work they do? It's character that counts."

"I don't care what he does. It's your life. Leave me out of it. '*Voir*.'"

Behind the hatch the Marmaladey quietly tidied. She'd said no word to me yet. Her toaster hummed each time a piece popped up. Bridie tucked her sandwich away, the paper making a little crackle. She wouldn't be in for tea tonight. She left, smiling a faraway smile.

When they had both gone I went into the Marmaladey's kitchen to inspect it for cleanliness. I'd never seen such an immaculate workplace. The plates were already rinsed, tiles mopped, curtains neatly tied with mauve bows. An electric wall clock whirred, the fridge clicked on and off. I took a freshly ironed cloth to wipe the delft, arranging them where I thought best. Inside the fridge were butter, milk, eggs, and some marmalade jars. The food was little different from the food at home, the kitchens were worlds apart, this was a holy place. Her new mop was speckless, fluffy. I watered the plant on her windowsill, watching the drops run down the stalks. Besides the plant was a dish of warm custard. I tasted it. I put some on a saucer.

"Come, Biddy. Out. They've gone. Taste this."

Again she'd spent the night up on my pillow. Light made no difference to her. I'd woken, again to the smell of her feathers pushed into my face. Her beak tapped the saucer quickly. I went down for more custard. The third trip down, I brought the dish up. It was a golden custard, delicious. By the telephone in the mauve hall was a fat mauve pen, which I took up with me. "Dear Mammy. I have decided to stay here for good. I have a job where Eileen was. Keep well. Eve." A terse letter, it was the first I had written to her. Under the stamp I wrote S.A.G., for St. Anthony Guide, in best convent school fashion. I couldn't bring myself to include my father. I didn't know how to address him. The pen spattered a bit over the quilt. Eileen of the curls and unholy filth would like that. She would appreciate the room being turned into a henhouse. Once I had posted the letter, I wouldn't think of her so much. I wouldn't brood over the memory of wet fuchsia flowers, white petals on a tree, or rain-soaked hawthorn. The letter would help lay ghosts to rest. Mr. Canner's speckled hands would shake at the till, our hens would fly into the tree, Miss Taylor's lips would continue to spread gossip. I would forget. I was a city girl with a city boyfriend and a city job.

He hadn't tried to kiss me. As I stepped through the mauve gate he had pulled my hand, kissing the palm. His thin lips felt soft. I remembered the silkworms Mother Perpetua used to keep, feeding them mulberry leaves until the mulberry died and the silkworms disappeared from their boxes. I'd not thought of silkworms or entrusting a letter to the guidance of St. Anthony for years. His lips gave me a fuzzy feeling. I curled my fingers over the place they'd touched. He'd called out "Goodnight, madam" after me.

The telephone in the hall rang.

"Was it all right in the night? Was your hen quiet?"

"I wasn't late. Bridie came in after me. My landlady

snores. They're both at work now. Biddy ate something."

"Did she sleep or stay awake?"

"She won't become nocturnal. She seems to want to sleep a lot."

"They make their own pattern. She's not likely to break it. When do you leave for the job?"

"Half five. I am nervous."

"Don't be. I'll be there when you come out. What are you afraid of?"

"I might not be able for the work. I've only done shop work. In a chemist's. The owner was Bridie's father."

"If you did that you'll sail through a bit of cleaning." He added that it was maybe because I'd had the fall outside the new job that I was afraid of it. Nothing good came from fear. I was to remember him. He cared about me, cared what happened to me. I was to think of him waiting outside for me afterwards. Our voices exchanging sounds into the telephone strengthened our bond.

At tea I told the Marmaladey she looked tired, I wanted to be friends. She gave me an odd look, whispered that she looked forward to retirement, she'd like to give more time to her good clean home. She hoped I wasn't like my cousin. My Mam was a real lady or she'd not have risked taking me. She served slivers of boiled ham with a bottle of pickled onions. She wiped her long nose with small patting movements. Life was a lonely path for a single lady, even in Catholic Ireland. Would I be long eating? She shut the hatch with a bang, wanting her kitchen peace.

I wore my raincoat with the hood. I worried about being late as the bus swished through rainbow-colored puddles. The showrooms looked dead, unlighted, with no signs of cleaners. Red lamps were placed round the ropes cordoning off the road work. The men had gone, but for a night watchman in a little hut. I saw the tip of his boot through the door. I remembered my foot, which had stopped hurting since I danced with Skin. I wished I was going home, with a carefree evening planned like the students whizzing through the rain on their bikes, tingling their bells with impatient hands, their wet faces glowing above the yellow capes, the rain dripping from the oilskin hems. I envied the night watchman.

"Glory be tonight, is it youse again? Are you Miss Eve Joyne?"

Mrs. Carter's voice sounded behind me. For the third lucky time her teeth were smiling at me, this time from under a black umbrella, her curlers mixing with a bent tangle of spokes. She wore her cracked men's shoes.

"Mrs. Carter, you're not my boss, are you? I thought you worked at the station. Do you work here?"

"For this fifteen year or more. I left the station position, or it left me, you might say. I'm not a horse, I said. Glory. The long arm of coincidence."

"I can't believe it either."

"I told Dympna about you. About the girl from the country out looking for her cousin. Did you find her?"

I didn't feel anxious. I knew her, I was to work for the first one who had welcomed me, who I had wished to mother me. Regular cleaner, friend, she was my boss. I told her I hadn't found Eileen, I wasn't so worried about her now.

"I'd have put you more in the professional class, hairdresser maybe, or behind a counter somewhere."

"I had a fall. I landed up in hospital."

99

"Glory. What happened then?"

"I'm staying here and so I took this job. I'm staying in Drumcondra."

"Where your cousin stayed? What happened?"

"She went to England." Drumcondra started the swallowing of Eileen, England finished it. I wouldn't find her now.

"England? Bad place. Where my lads went. No loss to this country. Why the cleaning?"

"It was handy. That's all they offered."

"I'm right pleased. Come while I show you round."

She led me to a gray-painted passage smelling of wellingtons where I hung my coat. I felt at peace. I'd polish ceilings for Mrs. Carter, new boss-mother showing me the ropes. There was no polishing. She made it plain that there was little work.

"I don't believe in unnecessary labor. If I were to elucidate. . . . Glory, girl, you save your strength, never mind the work."

"What is necessary? What shall I do first?"

"We'll wet the tea first. That takes place first. Look, this is the kettle. I'll just give Dympna a ring while it's warming."

She talked rapidly into the receiver to Dympna with the people at the Mental, telling about the country girl, her with the gadabout dress who had come to work in the showrooms. She made a couple more calls, rubbing her tired eyes. One to a pub where C. Him might be found, another to a bookie about a particular horse. I asked again about the work.

"Glory, girl. Folk in this office want two things, a desk for their work and a chair. A telephone is handy. That's all we clean."

"That's all? You're sure?"

"Do you doubt my word? Turn out the ashtrays, a lick and a wipe. The girls eat apples with their mid-mornings when they talk into the telephone. Bun crumbs, powder too, the creatures. I empty the bins an odd time. A handy thing, a telephone. I don't see well, my eyes get tired. I like a telephone."

"Then what do we do?"

"Then? Why, your time is yours. Have you any person to ring up? A little chat. It passes the time grand."

Making calls was the main part of the night's work, it came first. She rang her sister in Cabra to discuss a recipe for apple cake. Then she got back to Dympna, who had caught a cold from the wet.

I wiped out a telphone, wondering if Eileen had eaten a bun into it or spat apple pips into the ashtray. No doubt she powdered her face often, having squeezed her spots. Probably she smoked too and blew smoke into laddos' faces. It was sad not to have anyone to ring.

Mrs. Carter made a strong pot. I asked if we had to scrub sometimes. She looked pitying.

"Go way out of that. The floors is of no consequence. A tidy desk for staff to use a telephone or write a letter an odd time is what is required."

The vacuum had broken years ago. When I asked about the corridors she didn't bother answering. Sometimes she wiped a chair. A wiped chair went down well with the staff.

The hot brown tea was pleasant after the rushed slices of thin ham in Drumcondra. We sat, our elbows on the desk, pouring, stirring, and talking. Mrs. Carter liked to amuse herself by dialing any number. "Hulloa, Mrs. Off? I'm Mrs. On." "This is Store Street Police. Tell Mr. Mogg the cat is here." "Is that Mr. Stench? What are you going to do about it?" A grand invention, the telephone. She also liked correspondence. A bill or a receipt was easy for eyes worn with hard work. She held them close under her nose. A letter from a consumer about gas supply was thrilling. She relished a complaint. Real people wanted gas for cookers that didn't cook, wrote to complain. Real people wanted more gas, having not paid for that previously used. Real people wanted heat for their grand homes. She had great sympathy for those financially embarrassed, without the ready to make a pot of tea, she knew that road. She liked to know the whys and wherefores, money problems of her own citizens, rooting through In trays, her mouth set happily round her black teeth. Out trays were not so fascinating. She liked problems, cries of outrage.

With telephoning, reading, and tea drinking, the time went fast. I smoked three of her cigarettes and felt citified. She told me about Dympna. Classed as retarded, she was capable only of little jobs around the Mental Hospital. She would have liked her home but she was too much all day and every day, the mentals were a godsend, keeping Dympna busy, housing her. Dympna never got a fellow. Had I found one, here in the city?

"I did meet someone."

"Where?"

"The dance last night."

"Didn't I tell you? It was the gadabout dress. I well remember I wore red the night I met C. Him. Dancing and a bit of red. Mind, I never let him lay a finger on me till the ring was on. You are a Catholic?"

"I . . . yes. I went to a convent."

"Catholic. Faith is the best precaution, puts the fear in you if you get tempted. He's Catholic too?"

102

"I don't know. He loves nature. He buys and sells . . . food . . . for animals."

I didn't know his real name, much less his faith or origin.

Mrs. Carter removed her nose from a letter about a debt. His job was of no matter, if he paid his way. Religion was important, faith was a precautionary measure, kept you right. If my fellow was meeting me, we might as well pack up. We arranged the unused buckets, dustpans, and brooms around the broken vacuum, swilled out the pot and teacups. She got her old umbrella. Another evening had passed, my company made it a lot more pleasant. She didn't regret the station job, they asked too much. Instead of feeling exhausted as I had feared, I felt fresh and lively. I'd get myself some friends. Each night the showrooms would buzz with conversations dialed by myself and my new boss-mother.

And Skin was there. He waited quietly, his elbows protruding slightly. The angle of his head, his slightly pointed ears, reminded me of a bird ready for flight, a strong, wise bird. I forgot Mrs. Carter, waiting to be introduced, leaving her under her broken umbrella with her hand outstretched. There was just Skin and myself, together again, hands held, moving away. He put his face to mine. His nose had a tiny scar over the left nostril.

"Happy, dear one? Was it all right?"

"I knew her. I knew my boss. I met her before, when I first got here."

"You should have introduced me."

"I forgot."

I turned, in time to see Mrs. Carter's umbrella disappearing round the corner.

"The work wasn't too hard?"

"It was nothing. That's where I fell, back there. Look."

"I know. I saw. I've been waiting half an hour."

He told me as we walked about his own fear of falling, a fear acquired early when he accompanied his guardian to the city. His guardian left the tinkers, had taken to the city to be a skin man. Skin picked up the trade from his guardian, who'd been a violent man, in rages he would push Skin from the cart. That's how he got the scar, had I noticed? His guardian had taught him to harness up, to drive the cart standing. Skin would get hit if he didn't hold the leather reins correctly, hit for dawdling. He hated and feared falling. Falling was a dying sensation, you lost control. That's why he had particular sympathy for me and my trouble. His guardian had died, Skin took over the route, determined to succeed, do something better with his life one day. He didn't mix with his fellows, a rough lot of characters. He was not a snob, though. He knew nothing of his parents. His guardian had done his best, he held no ill will.

"What do you wish, Skin? What would you most like?"

"To be a travel agent. I want my own business. To be able to board a plane, see for myself. Can you understand?"

"Of course. That's what I'd like. You don't hate your guardian?"

"Not hatred. Contempt perhaps. He couldn't help himself. It's hard to change your nature. He lacked any ambition. He cared for me in his fashion."

"I hated my father. I still do."

"Try not. Hate destroys. It is negative."

"It's why I left. Because of him. And to find Eileen, of course. I must find her."

"It would seem she doesn't need you. Let her go, Eve, think of yourself. She hasn't tried to contact you. You have your own life."

His quiet voice was truthful. Eileen was gone for good, she didn't want me, like Bridie. I was deluding myself. I'd never find her, she was like the elusive pot of gold at the end of the rainbow, not wanting to be found. Skin was good and wise, knowing about birds, and knowing about people.

We took another way home, hurrying through side streets. He held me against him. Nothing mattered except that we were close. His skin was rough from rough weather, rough work, the handling of rough reins and grooming his brown horse. He had to haul buckets of refuse, but he smelled lovely, of fresh air and health. His thin hands felt strong and comforting. The nails were clipped short, clean. He half lifted me across puddles, the tips of his slightly pointy ears rosy in the damp. An Adam's apple bobbed in his thin neck when he talked. Talking as fast as he moved, he told me he'd never been a great mixer. His work was a means to an end. He read a lot. Did I enjoy James Stephens? Why had I left school?

"I felt I had to. I had to leave home."

"No small ambition to relinquish. You let go of a good chance."

"You don't understand. There was my brother too. The cost of it. It was too much to bear."

"Tell me."

I told him about the night Maxie went to the General, to stay forever possibly. All our efforts had been wasted, the pills, the tying, the watchfulness, all wasted, he was beyond help. Without us, alone with my father and her glittering watch, I'd seen my mother happier than she had ever been. I wanted no children, if I ever married. I didn't want to teach.

"Life can be a hard teacher. Your time has been hard."

He said I was right to make up my own mind, not go against my instinct. When we reached the mauve gate he waited, leaning his elbows on it. Would I think of him as steady? He wanted our relationship to be taken seriously. Did I mind his work? Could I put up with it until he was able to better himself? I was so beautiful.

"Put up with you? You've saved me. You and Mrs. Carter have made everything different. It was terrible before."

"I'll be there tomorrow. In the same place by the showrooms."

He brushed my face with his flat cheekbones that narrowed to a narrow chin. I wasn't frightened. He pushed the gate, his arms went round, and I wasn't frightened. Skin made me forget fright with his pointed friendly face, his kisses. I wanted him to go on kissing me but he told me to go in, he'd watch me go through the door. My heels made no sound on the wet stones by the leering gnomes and dead roses.

Inside was the Marmaladey, her face gone pinched and small, her eyes iced with hatred.

"Shall I lock the door? Is Bridie in?"

I had expected her to be snoring. Instead she stood looking at me fiercely.

"Bridie is not in, miss. It's not Bridie I'm wanting. It's you, miss."

"What have I done?"

Apart from her whispering about retirement, this was

our first conversation. The face was hard now, a wrinkled enemy with a lot to say.

"I've been. I've seen. I've went up and I've seen."

"What have you seen?"

"I've seen the electric light. My good electric left wasting. Is that what your mother paid for, for waste of good light?"

"I'll pay. I'm sorry."

"What use is 'sorry'? What use is payment? No use whatsoever. The bird then, what about the bird?"

"Bird? Did a bird get in?"

I licked my lips, different-tasting after Skin's kisses. I wanted him. The fright was coming back.

"You know well what bird. A great farm bird, miss. Sitting on my good pillow. Soiling the good bed. I don't rent beds for birds. I saw with my own eyes."

"I'm sorry. I will pay."

"Pay? And what about that box? Don't think I missed it, nasty thing. Great nasty box on my carpet, soiling it, all mess and feathers. You're no better than your cousin, the two of you's tarred with the same dirt. What have you to say?"

"Nothing. I will pay."

"You're wicked. Worse than your cousin, you're unnatural. I should have known better, only your mother, a real lady, begged me."

"She paid you. That counts, doesn't it?"

"The bold lip of you, worse than your cousin. A farm bird in the bed, it's not natural. Your cousin stole, owed rent, you're worse. You stole my pen, you stole my good cream custard. Hens in the bed. Custards. Now get you out."

"Out where? I'm sorry. I will pay."

She raised a crooked hand as if to scratch me. Her

107

dark mauve toque had slipped to show her hair pinned like a thin cockscomb. Out.

I banged the door. I ran back up the paving stones away from the one with the clawed hand. I called to Skin, just visible at the end of the wet black road.

"Skin, wait. Wait."

"What is it, dear? I'm here. Quiet now."

"She found her. The Marmaladey found her. I have to leave. I'm to get out."

"Marmaladey?"

"The landlady. She found Biddy."

"Calm down. I'm here. I will protect you. There."

"Where shall I go?"

It was worse than Maxie, worse than my father or falling down a hole. I was done for.

"Lookit, Eve. Stop crying. I'm here, aren't I? Wait while I think."

He held me again, patting my arms gently. I must put up my rain hood. I must go back. I must stay there till morning. But I couldn't, I wouldn't do it. Yes, I must. Go quickly, before she barred the door, say nothing. My room was mine by right. Wait until morning. He'd come then, to fetch me, take me away. Remember, I was his own dear.

"Every creature must have space. Daylight, proper food, space to live, are basic rights for every living thing."

Skin disapproved of henhouses, curtailment of freedom. How could Biddy stay healthy with only a cardboard box and an airless bedroom? Electric light was no substitute for blue sky. Animals and human beings had their similarities. I'd done the best I could with her, trying to arrange my life round her, now he could help. No more egg custard, nothing sweet, a proper diet again.

He'd kept his word, arriving after Bridie and the Marmaladey left. At breakfast I'd found a note on the toast. My room was no longer available. I was requested to leave that day. There'd be no refund in view of the damage done by a hen. Mention was made of a cream custard, a pen, a ruined quilt. Bridie took no notice, efficiently making and wrapping her sandwich. She wiped the butter from her fingers on the cloth before sipping her tea. It wasn't her affair. Damian would propose soon, change was on the way for her too. I heard the toaster whirring behind the hatch for the last time.

He had a taxi waiting. He wore a thick sweater over the pants of his good suit. He wouldn't let me carry anything. His deep-set piercing eyes widened at the sight of such purple paint. Householders ought to take pride. The lady must have had a real fright in my bedroom. He carried Biddy last, inside her battered box. He applauded my initiative, but the plan was doomed, she would have died if this hadn't happened. Drumcondra would be a place of unhappy memory for me. I was glad to be leaving. Skin had never included the area in his rounds. That mauve was garish. Still, he approved of a neat place.

"I'll never see the color without thinking of this place."

"Through my work I've come to judge a householder's character by exteriors. I am a reasonable judge." Paintwork mattered, clean curtains, the state of gardens. Not a favorite part, Drumcondra.

"It sounds like a water snake."

"South American. The anaconda is a creature with a voracious appetite. It'll down a pig and look for more. I have an interest in snakes too."

"Where are we going now? Where are you taking me?"

"My place. It won't take long."

"Where you keep your horse? I am afraid of horses."

"The horse is stabled out in Cabra. I set off from there. I live in the city center. You will see."

No need to be scared of the horse, a short-legged gelding, gentle as a bird, no need in the world. Skin liked the heart of the city, away from where he worked, away from associates. He had his own hideout, where he wasn't known. He'd taken the day off to help me move.

"The people, Skin. Won't there be talk if I move in?"

"Talk is cheap. People the world over like scandal, thrive on it. They know me in my building."

What mattered was that I had somewhere to go, some kindness shown me after all I had been through. He'd not see me a vagrant.

"Thank you, Skin. Sometimes I believe in luck. You are my luck."

"And you mine."

His thin mouth smiled, close to mine in the back of the taxi, telling me I was his talisman, reassuring me. The smell of Biddy came through the holes in the box. Skin said he'd known when he saw me outside the church of the novenas that our futures would come together.

"But is there room?"

I was unsure of what he had in mind. Was I to become like a city girl in the pages of the magazines, scorning convention, defying the church's blessing? He didn't know me. Did he think I was green, or experienced? There was the problem of my underwear, still countrified and awful. He went on quietly speaking of his home. Of course there was room. Though a tenement, I'd like it. He had an affection for his city, I'd learn to love it too. By sharing we'd learn each other's ways.

"But . . . is it wrong?"

"Of course not. Why are you afraid?"

"I don't know. My family . . ."

"I thought you were independent. What you think matters, not convention. I'm not asking for anything you don't agree to."

"They . . ."

"They? Are 'they' to rule you?" If everyone was governed by "them" there'd be no change or progress.

111

"Were you happy as a child, Skin?"

"I try to forget the unhappy times."

He'd learned early to conceal his fear, to put a good face on life.

"I want to be like that. My mother doesn't care where I go now."

I would have liked to ask him about my bad period. It scared me. Blood scared me. Blood ought to stay in veins, out of the way, not dribble uncontrollably.

"Here, this is my place."

The taxi stopped. It was evident, he said, that I had a caring heart. My hen-keeping idea was ingenious. Now we would devise something better. Don't look at the outside of the building, wait till we get inside. I did see the rows of trash bins, awaiting collection behind some shabby railings. Skin said he could imagine my home in the country being clean. He imagined the kitchen had been welcoming, a place of neighborliness. Was I sure his work didn't disgust me?

"I'm not a snob. Your work matters, you should be proud. It is in any case a means to an end. You are ambitious. This house is big."

"Up to the top. The very top is mine. I'm fond of solitude."

Rubbish gushed over the edges of the bins, the steps were cracked down the center, split up to the door-frame. The door was without lock or handle, the letter-box a hole in the wood. Glass from the fanlight was gone, apart from a few jagged pieces. Someone had started to paint the lintel, had given up after a few smears. The paint had spilled. A dried white pool had been trodden in, white footmarks covering the boards, ascending the staircase, the white getting gradually fainter. There was no floor covering, most of the banisters were gone.

He went up first, carrying the box, feet echoing. Leave everything else, he'd come down later. He explained that the tenants were supposed to take turns cleaning the stairs. They argued and found fault, making excuses. Recently, rather than have ill feeling, Skin took the job over, a weekly scrub and no conflict. He'd change that old paint eventually, and see to the front door. A doorway was important, set the tone. The landlord was his personal friend, letting Skin have the top flat for a nominal sum, in return for services. He hadn't been there long. He liked the anonymity of the city center. He sensed my nervousness, going ahead with Biddy. We clattered across various landings, lit by rain-spattered windows and smelling of various dinners behind shabby doors. At the top he turned, eyes suddenly gone shy. He was embarrassed now of what I might think of his home.

"It's here."

The last flight had dark linoleum, dulled by layers of polish. The banisters were repaired. On the landing was a lavatory, the open doorway letting in light from a stained-glass window above the toilet. The red, blue, and dark panes shimmered with rain. Skin said he liked the window, surprising and churchlike at the very top, the light making a pretty effect. The landing had a fresh coat of white paint. He shut the lavatory door to muffle the glugging toilet, embarrassed slightly. There were two flats, this was his, here on the left.

More white paint, blinding white, with his bed the first object in sight, a monk's bed, narrow, without springs, stretched with a thin blanket. The corners were tucked neatly. He touched it. He didn't believe in soft living, liked austerity. What did I think? I looked at the wide wood shelf under his window, no ornament in sight. I looked at the bare light bulb hanging above the bed. There was a candle on the shelf, for studying.

"Where do you sit, Skin?"

"I don't. I'm used to the standing. The shelf is for my studies. I've grown to prefer standing. I like to keep moving. I lie down when I'm tired."

His books were everywhere, alphabetically stacked in piles to the ceiling. I'd never seen so many books outside a library, about natural history mostly. He mentioned his research into birds again. Ornithology was a delight that never failed. He touched the shelf. Had I known that Virginia Woolf worked standing? It came easily to him because of driving his horse. He kept pens and pencils in a round jar.

"It's nice and peaceful here."

I sat on his blanket, marveling. It was like no home I could imagine, with nothing but his bed and books and one shelf to work on. Where did he put his things? Where did he eat? He opened a narrow door, no wider than a cupboard behind the white curtains. His kitchen was a slit-sized place, the width of the sink only, with a skylight. There was a portable cooker with two shelves under it for clothes, shoes, and some cooking pots. The paint here was white too.

"It's beautiful. Er . . . where do I sleep, Skin?"

I was relieved that his bed was so narrow, two people couldn't sleep in it. I watched his hard wide cheeks, his chin, his thin lips smiling at me. What did he expect?

"I've planned everything. I'll buy some foam. Foam rubber makes a great mattress. I'll sleep in here, there's room. You take the bed."

114

I was relieved that he understood. We would stay apart until the time came, the right time, till we were ready. Divided by the thin white door, I would be private.

"No, Skin, it's your bed. You must stay in it. I'll take the foam. I keep forgetting your name is Oisin, do you mind?"

"Call me anything you wish. But I'll sleep in the kitchen."

Our relationship would flower gradually. We'd talk a lot, and touch. For my sake he'd chosen to give up his own bed, to sleep in discomfort with bony feet wedged into his kitchen door.

"Thanks."

"About the hen. I'll make a gate for her, hinged, to close in the top landing. With the toilet window open she'll have air and good running space. When did she last lay?"

"She never did. There's something wrong with her. She stayed small, didn't develop. I got fond of her for that."

"She may pick up. I've known it to happen. Good care, running space. Attention works miracles occasionally." He picked her up, smoothing her gently.

"But the people. In the flat across the landing. They might not like a hen scratching about, or a gate. They use the same lavatory?"

"There is no one. It's vacant. I converted it. I'm only after finishing the paint."

"Then I could rent it. I could move in if it is empty."

His face changed. He'd thought of it, but hadn't suggested it, because of wanting me as near as possible. It was the obvious move. Good for the bird too, to have the whole top floor. The landlord would agree, he would do anything for Skin. He might get it for a cheap rent. He had the key with him, we could look now. He'd tell the landlord when he collected the rents. He collected for the whole building. I smiled. I felt like dancing. My luck continued.

Skin was a man of real kindness, prepared to put me first, prepared to sleep in too short a space, to risk malicious tongues, prepared to house Biddy and cure her.

We crossed the white landing, heard the toilet gurgling through the closed door again. He opened the door to the right of the stairwell. I smelled more fresh paint. There was an old-fashioned grate with just a gas ring for cooking behind a tiled fender. The bed, a wider one, was under the window. I was pleased with the screen around the washbasin in the other corner, a place to wash privately. Never again the fear of being watched, of washing myself under attack. I needn't fear anyone, I could take my time, look at the pictures pinned to the screen, holy ones and scenes from holiday resorts. My new door had no bolts, I didn't mind. I wasn't afraid of Skin. There was a card table with a green baize top where we could take our food. I'd buy a cloth. I'd buy white candles. Up on the wall was an old-fashioned meat safe to keep food in. I'd make great plans while bending over the gas ring, plans for Skin's travel agency. One day I'd wear a bikini like Eileen, get tanned, travel with him.

"I hope you don't think the white monotonous. It's to attract light. We'll be happy here together. I could change the white."

"I love everything."

"We'll open all the windows. Biddy, my bird, you're in your paradise."

"Should we put paper down for her?"

116

"Not at all. We might even train her. In the meantime let her have space."

He put her gently to the floor. She stood still, warily. She lifted her head again, her expression prouder, more aloof, more like the old Biddy. Then she looked up, as if expecting to see tree branches, or white skirts dancing round bare legs. She was confident, her pinkish comb firmer, her eyes round with inquiry. Small and old-fashioned she was, the Biddy that I loved. I'd never cared for dolls. Doll houses, stuffed animals, and games weren't found in our home. Our toys had been hens in the orchard, our doll house the broken greenhouse where we invented games. I told Skin about Eileen and me singing, dancing, scattering grain over the birds. How we'd play with them, pretending they were human. He could understand her loss to me, how I must miss her.

"You'll meet her one day. You will."

"No, Eve, remember what I said. You must stop trying to trace her. You don't need her now. Nor Bridie."

"She may be missing me."

I tried to explain. Eileen was so lively, she had flourish and attack, she saw a joke. Why should I wipe her from my future? Surely we'd sing again, dance one day, laugh? It didn't matter about Bridie.

"Come back to my flat a minute. I've something you may like."

Under his electric hot plate he had a small record player. He liked music with a beat, to help when he practiced dancing. "Let's twist again, like we did last summer. Let's twist again, like we did last year, do you remember when things were really hummin'? Let's twist again, twisting time is here." He started moving, jerkily, his knees rather stiff. He liked this dance, liked watching it, but found it difficult. They'd stopped it now, it was old-fashioned, did I like it?

"Watch, Skin. Watch my knees. Relax on your feet, let your hips move. Slide on the ball of one foot like me."

He loosened gradually, starting to slide naturally, his socks making no sound on the boards. His hips swung right and left, countering his arm movements. Intent, he looked exalted. I started to love him then. His face, his laughing eyes, his hands with the long fingers were precious, to be treasured. His gaiety was partly born of sorrow, I guessed that. Being close to him, living closely, sharing closely, would increase love. I knew he loved me. He moved out of his flat again, still dancing. He'd got the trick of it now, his angular body writhing across the white landing with me following. He was the clurichaun holding the pot of gold, catch him. Quickly. If you got the gold you'd be immortal. Dodging this way, that way, fast and magical, made me forget trouble. He stretched his long hands over Biddy. I tried to grab him.

"Lookit, Eve. Look at the bird."

Biddy hopped now in a lively way. The music braced her, lifted up her heart. She raised her yellow claws, flourishing them with a sideways kick, her kind of a dance, keeping near us. Skin didn't let me catch him. We saw Biddy tap with her beak while she moved, pecking at various surfaces, a book, the tin dish he'd put down for her water, the floorboards. The needle stuck then. "Let's twist, let's twist, let's twist." We laughed, not caring, nothing mattered, safe in our charmed circle, safe in the white top floor, safe with the books and music. I caught him. He put his arm round me. Then we danced close, my breasts pressed against his chest, feeling his heart near, beating under his bawneen sweater, beating clear.

"You've changed everything for me, Eve. I had no one before."

"You didn't?"

"I did not. You're lovelier. You're lovelier than everyone."

He pulled me to the cupboard with the stained mirror in it. Now the big-busted girl had a boy with her, pulling her back to him, a tall, thin, laughing boy, a boy with a bony chin and most unusual ears.

"Do you really think so? My bust isn't . . . isn't too big, is it?"

"To me it's perfect."

"Eileen used to tease me."

"Jealous. You're perfect everywhere. You're sure about the walls? You might get tired of them."

"I won't. I love them."

He hugged me. He called me his flower. A no-name flower, the loveliest of all, a flower in early bloom.

"Which flowers do you love, Skin? Which is your favorite?"

I wanted to grow them, his favorites, here in the house. I'd have them on the white landing by the lavatory, flowers in red, blue, and dark colors matching the stained glass. The landing would be a bright bower, flowery and light, containing a hen bird.

"I like anemones, the garden kind with rich colors and black stamens. They have black pollen."

He liked the wild ones too, so fragile, windpollinated, white. I was a wild wood anemone. Then there was the Japanese variety, pale pink or white on long stalks with lemon-colored centers, found in old

119

gardens. He'd thought of anemones when he first saw my bright dress, not the color, but the way I moved, gracefully.

He let go of me to see to the record player. Again, light-footed, sure, shrugging his thin shoulders, he danced away from me. He called out questioning me about boyfriends, had I had many?

"Nobody proper. There was a man. In May. English."

"Blind to have left you. You will like it here. This place is bare because I like plain ways. You can have anything. Are you good at cooking?"

"I never tried a lot."

"Everyone should be able. It keeps you healthy, right food is important."

"What time is it?"

"I'll see you to your job in time, don't fear."

"I thought of not going. After the move. The upset."

"But you must. You only just started, you're committed."

A job was a responsibility, you were obliged. He didn't mean the money, he earned plenty for us both. I'd given my word to my employers. Trust mattered. By working overtime he hoped to start on his own in two years or so, start his travel agency. Did I like traveling?

"This is my first move. I never left before."

"I know Ireland. Nowhere else."

All that would change when he started his business. He looked serious. I saw our future. I'd be there, beside him, giving him support in a clean, well-lighted office, with walls pinned with enticing pictures, of places he'd like clients to go to, places he knew, sunny places, places with high mountains, flowery or snowcapped, skyscrapers in a megalopolis. We'd be comfortable. He could work standing or sit peacefully when he got tired. I'd wear his ring one day. I wanted no children. The business and our clients smiling at us would be enough.

"I'd like to see you working. Can I come with you when you take the cart?"

"Surely. You could stay with the horse while I collect. It's heavy, handling the pails."

He'd lend me one of his own coveralls, a cap to tuck my hair under. I'd be his mate, dressed in his own clothes. He'd teach me the special cry to call through the city outskirts, heralding his approach. His job taught him much about human nature, all grist for his ambition.

I unpacked while he got a meal ready, to eat before I left. Quantities of wire coat hangers jangled when I opened the cupboard door. There was a camphor smell there, and a child's white wool sock. Skin thought it strange, he'd heard of no youngster living there. I looked again in the stained mirror, at my white face, my hand holding the white wool sock. From Skin's flat came smells of cheese toasting. In my grate were pieces of half-burned coal, ash powdering the bars. Above it was the Sacred Heart, quiet, gentle-faced. The frame and glass were blackened, my finger came away black. Skin got a cloth. He'd forgotten to wipe it after doing the place, sad to have the holy face spoiled, he'd forgotten to clean it after decorating. He rubbed carefully. Soon it would be time to leave. How did I like my eggs? We'd eat another snack later. I didn't want him to know that I'd never cooked anything except scraps for poultry. I didn't want him to know about the outhouse, the leaky roof, the bath and other things. I wanted to be like him, wise, a good counselor, a person to turn to, interested in self-improvement. I looked forward to get-

121

ting home to the flat again, sure of him, not tense any more.

"Another ten minutes and we'll go."

He kissed with his eyes open. His tongue and his eyes joined mine. I wondered why I'd ever been afraid. Kissing wasn't hard. The present mattered, forget the past, don't think of the unknown future, only now counted. The slobbers of the postman's son, Matthew's expertise under the apple tree, Eileen's giggling, overheard jealously from my bedroom, the straggled moustache, vile-smelling, containing broken teeth, had all been fearful. This was delight. He held my face, alone and loving, alone and belonging. Meeting with the mouth was the heart's exploration. He asked nothing that I didn't ask myself. We kissed a long time on the bed under the window. My love, my dancing kissing man, made me late for work in spite of his talk of responsibility and jobs.

"Glory be tonight, you look half moonstruck. Have a cupeen."

"I'm sorry, Mrs. Carter, to be late."

"What about it? If I were to elucidate . . ."

"I've moved. I've moved from Drumcondra. I'm . . . I am in . . ." I felt absurd again, not knowing the name of my new street. The street and house number was the first requirement of city dwelling. At home your name would find you.

"What was wrong with the other place? All mauvey and done up, your landlady sounded a nice sort. First your cousin, then you take off from it. You country ones have big ideas."

"The boy I met . . . I told you. He found me a place. Somewhere more central."

"You didn't introduce me. I don't bear malice. Wait, girl, till you're wed. I'll look into your tea leaves."

She had made her telephone calls, now was the time for cup reading. She swirled the dregs vigorously, nothing like a good swirl round for a true forecast. She peered closely, blinking her tired eyes. Happy, was I? Happy with my new feller? I was on the verge of change. There was some kind of a ring ahead, or a bell maybe, but not yet. There was something . . . yes, something not right. No wedding yet. I wasn't doing wrong, was I, not going the wrong way? And I a Catholic.

"Of coure I'm not. I am surprised, Mrs. Carter, that you should think it."

"There is something. Something a quare shape altogether, something you might see stuffed. A big stuffed thing." She leaned further, her eyes red-rimmed.

"Stuffed? What do you mean, stuffed?"

"Something like in a museum."

She'd taken her children once, years back, to a museum in the city. The sight of those stuffed animals preyed on her for many a week after. Educational, she'd grant. For recreation she'd sooner have tea and the telephone.

"What else is there?"

"Water. A deal of wet."

"That's nothing new. Look, still lashing down."

"The rain gives me a fever in the joints. There's been few sunny days in my little life. There's no sense in chasing happiness. You won't find it, not for long. You just get old. If I were to . . . I'll just give Dympna another ring, see if it's raining still, out at the Mental. Then we'll pack up."

I wiped an ashtray. Was she right about happiness?

123

Everyone expected it, who, that I knew, had found it? I thought of Mr. Canner again, his mind whiskey-fogged, talking about cloud catching. I sipped some leather-colored tea. Mrs. Carter rubbed at her eyes. She'd like to meet my bloke.

I rinsed out the cup with the quare beast in it. Skin made me happy.

He was outside, waiting with his cart and brown horse as a surprise. Behind his neat-stacked pails and shining bins was a brown paper parcel. He thought it would please me to see him in his work get up again. He put his hand out to shake Mrs. Carter's, he'd gladly give her a lift home if she wished it.

"The beast, the beast, the quare size of it, I saw it, 'tis the beast inside the cup."

Mrs. Carter bounded forward, ignoring Skin's hand. She loved any kind of a horse, here was a lovely great brown beast with a soft nose, waiting to take her home. She tripped, she knocked the shaft pole, there was a great clatter. The horse's hooves slipped on the wet road, he lurched, lunging with his back legs. Slowly the cart tipped. Skin put his weight against it, pushing, trying to pacify his horse. Hey up, Malone, easy there, easy. Mrs. Carter screamed as she went sprawling into the wet under the clattering hooves. Glory, the beast, the beast, ready to ruin her entirely. Skin pushed harder as the cart tipped further. The pails clashed, the huge brown parcel fell into the road. It was then Skin got the kick. He lay by Mrs. Carter, who shrieked without stopping. He lay quietly. The rain beat on the paper parcel, showing the bars of a shiny bird cage near the hole in the road.

"Can I help you?"

I wouldn't say "madam." It was demeaning. Not even to please Mrs. Quest, my supervisor. She was the opposite of Mr. Killem. At Killem's no customer had been sirred or madamed. It would have been laughed at. I'm sure my father wouldn't often say "sir" to one of his town customers. The metropolis was different. Staff here had to be humble, it was expected. Humility was a requirement in this grand store. You asked hundreds of times each day if you could help faces that paused at the counter. I didn't like the work. It was a matter of trying to forget, of working hard, of asking each rich blank face if I could help it. I must block out the old times, think about the new, not think of Mrs. Carter wailing, block out the shouting at the ambulance men. "Leave him, leave him alone. There's nothing you can do. Can you not see? The bloke is dead. Kicked to death by his own brown horse." She'd gone on keening, keened for hours. She'd seen it in the cup. Little did she anticipate the beast would be Eve's feller's own brown horse. She'd only run to stroke its nose, the soft big size of it all wet in the rain. Her fond of a horse. She'd placed many a pound for C. Him on horses over the years. You couldn't be up to them when it came to rac-

125

ing, but a horse was incapable of badness, not planned badness. The beast had took exception to having his nose touched. Glory, if the cup had but elucidated.

"Can I help you? Toilet water? On the perfume bar, not on this counter."

Mrs. Quest knows I'm not happy. That I do not fit. She's got an Irish husband, knows that we're different. She is kind. She mustn't show favoritism, but there are rules. I'm not in lax Ireland now, I've emigrated like Mrs. Carter's no-good lads, I've left. Skin's dead to me at present, he won't be dead forever. I must believe that, I do believe. He'll live, he won't die and be buried. "Whisht now, give over that," the men said, leaning over him, pushing Mrs. Carter aside. Stop that blathering about brown horses, the kicked chap was alive, stop that. Hurt bad, yes, hurt very bad, much more and he'd have gone. Alive, stop that.

"Can I help? Something flowery? A flower scent? These are all French."

The perfumes are costly, nothing under ten pounds. Mrs. Quest is a kind boss, but wants me to say madam. I will not. The rest, the cockneys on the perfume bar, won't talk, will not include me, the new Irish assistant. Why should I abase myself for the sake of the perfumery till? This essence sells at twenty pounds, that yellow one fifteen. They shade variously from glaucous green to pale honey. I never heard of any of these brands. At Killem's it was lavender or rose water, nothing French. I'll not say madam, I'm no servant, I'm Eve. You, and you over there, you, I'm Eve, don't change me. Madam, I'm Adam. It is vital to please Mrs. Quest, I owe the job to her. A job is a commitment. Do not think of Skin. I am reliable. I must sell many bottles, fill the till, forget. His spine is damaged, but not mortally, kicked in his vertebrae by his own brown horse, the horse he named Malone. I will not say madam.

"Can I help you?"

Grave accidents take time, hospitalization over a long period. The doctor in the intensive-care ward asked who were his relatives? A tinker, was he? Had he an address? Mrs. Carter explained I was his financey, deal with me. Financeys came top of the relation list. Tinker he might be, he was my bloke whose cart had the misfortune to stick in the very hole I'd fallen in before. His cart and horse had done a mischief, I was nearly without my bloke. I wasn't to go back to that quare place on my own, that quare white flat I'd told about, a cupboard with a child's sock and no comfort, I was to stay with them. My wish came true, I became a Carter, one of the Carter family. For a time I shared a bed with the schoolies. Their clothing stained with porridge, their tangled hair, their silence became part of my life. They wore their shoes in bed, whispering quietly in the dark.

"Can I help, please? 'Quleques Fleurs'? What kind of flowers?"

Mrs. Quest is patient, doesn't mind questions, bears with my mistakes. There is a lot to learn. She gave me the key to the locked showcase, to show her trust in me, only I have the key. The choicest bottles are in my care. Which flowers? Apple blossoms? Mayflowers? Red fuchsia flowers? I'd like to see a Japanese anemone. The white landing will stay bare, no flowers to please and delight Skin. I'm in another land. And Mrs. Quest is watching me. I ought to know the stock now. I ought to stop thinking, live in the present. Mrs. Carter screamed when she saw Biddy. She came with me to the white flat for my things. She'd not anticipated hens, a hen was a quare object for a bed. Could it be Biddy she'd forecast in the cup? She'd picked her up, and there was the egg. After one night on Skin's bed she'd laid her first egg, small, soft-shelled, but an egg, she'd laid before she'd seen her shiny new coop. Skin, lover of gulls and nightbirds, had worked a small miracle. The soft-shelled egg enraptured Mrs. Carter. Why had I not said? A hen was just what the Carters needed, luck for their own backyard, luck for the Carter breakfasts. The coop would be handy for the egg a day. They'd each have an egg in turn. If my bloke was going to revive, I must stay there till he came out, I must be one of them. No need to complain now, with Dympna away I had a place at the Carters'.

"Can I help? Chanel?"

"Eve. Try to remember to say madam, please."

"Yes, Mrs. Quest." But I'll not, not for this store or anyone. Madam, I'm Adam, but you see I'm Eve. This store is a sophisticated place, nothing cheap here. And I do not fit. I didn't fit at the Carters'. I tried to replace Dympna. It was her Thursdays. On Thursdays all the Carters changed. On Thursdays Dympna was the star, I wasn't wanted. Mrs. Carter started keeping back the daily egg, no one benefited at breakfast, the eggs must be for Dympna. Dympna looked cold when she saw me, snatching the eggs. She might be good with mentals, she wasn't good at home. They doted on her. For three months I was a Carter, one yet not one of them, dreading Dympna's Thursdays. On Thursdays I was on sufferance. On Thursdays I dreaded those mad eyes peering round the door under a silly hat, wanting eggs and attention. On Thursdays Mrs. Carter took her hair out of the metal curlers and she had a wash. She asked if

I'd mind going alone to the job on Thursdays, no one would know. Would I do her work on Thursdays, a return for kindness? She'd done a lot for me. The schoolies looped round Dympna, staring up under her hat brim, wanting endearments, wanting her smile, having poked Biddy in her coop in the backyard with a stick. It wasn't cozy in the showrooms on Thursdays, with no one to telephone except the intensive-care ward, which had no news. I cleaned a little, secretly, feeling disloyal to Mrs. Carter who'd never washed a floor. I tried to fix the vacuum.

Then Biddy stopped laying, small soft-shelled eggs ceased to come out of her. Each morning Mrs. Carter inspected the shiny coop, angrily lifting Biddy, angrily thumping her down. No egg. No tidbit in the Carter backyard. The bird wasn't cooperating, the bird was cheating. Glory, there was ingratitude. The bird had laid in the beginning, laid to get acceptance, had got tired of it. Then she turned on me. It wasn't the bird cheating, it was me. I'd stole the bird's eggs, that was the way of it. Jealous of her Dympna, I'd stole her eggs. Thieving was in my blood. Hadn't I told her with my own mouth about the egg custard, about a pen in Drumcondra, and my naughty cousin. Blood told, made itself evident. She'd been tolerant, had shown sympathy, thanks to herself I had a home, in clover with the Carter family. I was abusing kindness, stealing. What was I doing with the eggs? Without the egg the bird was useless. No egg, no hen. I said nothing. I hated Dympna. I'd go.

I sat by Skin's bed in the hospital. A nurse remembered me from the time of my fall, not with approval. I looked at Skin, white on the pillow, drawn-looking, the creases deeper round his eyes, looking for some kind of sign. Did he need me? What use was I to him? He was unconscious. I couldn't stay on at the cleaning job until he recovered. I couldn't stay on at the Carters'. I could travel now, use the time fruitfully. I thought his mouth moved. There, the nurse said, he may be trying to convey something, he's not uttered yet. It was too early for change, but a fiancée was a help in sickness, sitting with the inert patient while the staff worked for a better purpose. His speech, his hearing, his eyesight were affected by the gelding's hoof. His lips had moved. He was trying to speak a word. "Gravel," was it? He was trying to say "travel"? I saw his tongue tip. "Travel." This was my sign. Skin wanted me to travel. I'd go, I'd learn about the world for him, till he was well enough to work. I'd not go far, just over the water, use his recovery time usefully. I could thank Malone for my emigration.

Mrs. Carter apologized. She regretted her hastiness. She'd changed her mind entirely, asking humbly if I'd reconsider. And what about Biddy, what would happen now, poor little bird? Stay, wouldn't I, I was a handy extra daughter to have round. Reconsider. I told her I'd leave Biddy, she'd put up with enough moving, she could keep her. Mrs. Carter would mourn me, C. Him would miss my face, listening at table to his talk of horses, betting fancies. The schoolies would have the bed to themselves again. I'd never teach children.

"Can I help you? Body lotion? On the perfume bar, further along."

The smallest bottle in the locked cabinet is three inches high, the largest three feet six inches. They have the money here for frivolity, the English know little want. They organize labor, their welfare services distribute wealth scrupulously. The rich come here, sniff at the perfumes, idle and moneyed. And Mrs. Carter begged. She'd cried at the end, without dignity. She'd miss my cup, reading my future, miss possible further signs of quare beasts, rings. Had she not seen Malone, dead now from the fall, made into glue, probably, or pet food? On reconsideration she thought that first beast might have been a dodo, a prehistoric bird with small wings, seen in the museum, a dodo, not a horse. Could it have been a phoenix? If only I'd stay there, I would find someone else to ring from the showroom, another bloke, or even Dympna. Dympna didn't hate me, not at all. And I was no thief. An egg, a pen, what did it matter, please forgive, it was her time of life. She'd spoke before she thought. The schoolies had grinned, wanting to see me off, to wave to me from the quayside. Mrs. Carter had brought Union Jacks cut out from paper, to see me away in style. I'd kissed the tops of the schoolies' tousled heads, kissed Mrs. Carter's curlers, asking them not to linger, goodbyes were upsetting. Afterward, when they had gone, I found a mug in with my underclothes, with my name on it, painted unevenly in nail polish from a showroom desk. She swore to communicate, to pass on the news from the hospital, about my Skin bloke. I drank from her mug at the hostel where I had accommodation, waiting for a letter with a gas showroom heading, a letter of any kind. Then I wrote to the sister in charge of the intensive-care ward. Mr. Oisin Bohan was holding his own still, no change in his condition.

"Can I help? Umbrellas? First left, then on past the glove counter."

Mrs. Quest likes us to be helpful, to smile, to point a direction. Goodwill paves the way. A future purchase is encouraged by a smiled "madam" and a pointed finger.

The perfumery lures impulse buyers. They pause, beguiled by lovely smells, baited by tester bottles. They spray, they sigh, they sniff lovingly at their wrists, into the crooks of their elbows. They leave with each finger, the lobe of each ear, giving a different smell. They linger to look at a glove, put on a hat, considering. They come back to buy, expecting to be called madam. I won't say it. They take notes of high denomination from stuffed wallets, ensuring their continuing fragrance. A scent will enchant a man, a scent will keep a man. Men are ensnared by scent. I've changed. I must hold down this job. Ma Griffe, Cloud Heavenly, Lilith, Oiseau de Feu, all here in my locked closet. Cheaper brands, colognes, the toilet waters, are on the perfume bar, sold by the cockneys. Mrs. Quest likes me to remember the names of regular customers. She sees to the sales slips, keeps a check. There is a streamlined till.

"Can I help you, please?"

Mrs. Carter and her schoolies had brandished their little flags. My last remembrance of my own country was flags of this country and the rain falling. After I'd kissed them I went up the gangplank to sit in the cabin, where travelers were vomiting in anticipation, before the boat cast off. The heaviest swell in years, the girl in the bunk above moaned, regretting her one-way ticket. The intolerable hot summer, the wettest winter, the intolerable heaving seas. The swells made the floor tip. Passengers missed basins, powerless, feet slipping, mouths blaspheming the saints in heaven before they spat sick. I had no saint in heaven, I was alone, wiping my shoes on newspaper, pleased with my varnished mug. Loving and missing, loving and losing, was one of life's condi-

132

tions. I thought of Skin a lot. I must concentrate, I must exist delicately, I must listen.

"I'm sorry, Mrs. Quest, what did you ask me?"

I'd found the hostel, cheap accommodation, having asked. I share with Omega, another one like me, but black. The other girls have friends, but I am Irish, Omega is black, not popular. I'm pleased to have the job. This store takes cleaning seriously. I open the locked case, the flacons are my specialty. No pushing dust indifferently, no casual wiping here, surfaces must sparkle. There is a spray cleaner for glass cases, polish for wood. The till must be kept tidy, everything in order, new rolls inserted, with ink pads that stain the skin. Mrs. Quest likes hands to be well tended, hair neat and unfussy. She has tender, tired eyes and asks about my life. She mustn't show favoritism. Her eyes show that she has love from her Irish husband, to give and to receive. I'm a dreamer, she says, I dream and move too slowly. I should say madam and speak clearly. She knows and loves Ireland, the country of her husband, meanwhile my customers are my priority. A smile, a clear sentence, clean and quick service, are her rules. I have a knack for display, she lets me dress the cases, gives me a free rein.

I have a bag now, like Bridie, with me at all times, but no lipsticky letters or impedimenta. There was money under my pillow when I moved from the white flat, put there by Skin, in an envelope with my name. I kept that, to have his handwriting. Just my name and him touching it. I didn't cry over his accident, too shocked by his white face. I cried over his envelope. I kept it at the Carters', till the schoolies got it. I didn't cry as the boat left. Now, sharing with Omega, her

133

crying keeps me awake. Worse than the giggling schoolies is Omega's horrid noise.

The hostel girls are like the perfume-bar ones,
strange, with brash talk, weird sense of a joke. The girls
hang their wet underwear from the windows. Colored
shapes drip onto the heads of pedestrians, a hazard in
icy weather. You hear the noise of the hostel girls before you turn the corner, you see strangely decorated
sills. Noise, panties, the smell of chips hit you. These
metropolis streets are mean, as gray and secretive as the
faces in them, faces that rarely smile. They show a
blank endurance. There are many black faces, like Omega's, the laughter has been wiped off. I'll leave the
hostel, rent a bed-sitter, Omega will come with me, we
will support each other. We will leave the windows
hung with many-colored rags, we'll make our own nest.
I must work well, I will save. Mrs. Quest says I lack
confidence, that I'm unambitious. Status and qualifica-
tions matter in the metropolis. Mrs. Quest has aspira-
tions, her job as buyer is part of her business training.
She sorts papers efficiently, has no time for slackness.

I wrote to Mrs. Carter, wanting more news of Skin,
news about Biddy. Metropolis people slot letters into
boxes, confident of reply. Omega gets nothing either.
On Sundays we take bus trips. I compare the streets,
the people's faces, with those back in the city. No man
is an island, I need Omega. I need Mrs. Quest to look
at me with kind eyes. I need a letter.

"Can I help you?"

Mrs. Quest is watching again. She'll say something
again about "madam." I will not grovel. I'll set no store
by accent, social denomination, income, I judge by
character. Forget Ireland. I don't want to forget. Forget
Skin. I need him. I will be patient with the customers

who spray their upper-class hairlines with my merchandise, considerately offering the green and yellow essences that make their lives smoother. I'll give good service to the store that caters to the needs of a lifetime and after it. You can live here without going out. A library, a bank, a mortician, food, furniture, and clothing, bodily or mental requirements on sale if you have cash. They don't sell friends, though, in this microcosmic world. The store would prosper throughout slumps, recessions, earthquakes, our clean, well-tended hands would carry on. Mrs. Quest arranges our coffee breaks, totals commissions earned, sees that we're punctual, considerate for the sake of the store's profits. She may be Catholic. The cockneys are concerned with boyfriends, they dance, they drink in pubs, dominated by the chasing of boyfriends. Skin, wake from your hospital bed, take me out dancing, live with me. This place is sub-zero. The pipes in the hostel freeze nightly, the streets stretch on forever. I miss green buses, green telephone booths, Irish street signs, friendliness. I even miss Irish rain. Somewhere there is Eileen. Somewhere are Mrs. Carter's no-good lads. I only want Skin.

Mrs. Quest is going to speak. Another customer. I won't say it. I am Eve. I will not look.

"Can I help you, madam?"

"Madam? I'm not a madam. Don't you remember me, Eve?"

"It's . . . You're Matthew. It's you. Are you Matthew?"

"Yes. I'm Matthew."

The man standing by the showcase had a fuller face, a soft moustache now, seeming less tall than when we'd met last year. He touched the glass with a round forefinger and smiled. Matthew the dentist was here. Not seen since May, forgotten since I left the village, back again, looking at me with interest, wearing a dapper coat. I forgot all the things that had happened. I forgot Eileen, forgot why I had run, forgot falling and Skin's accident, forgot the Carters. Matthew was looking at me with those round eyes. I'd danced in a white dress and his mouth had smiled. That smiling mouth that had kissed me was smiling again in the store, his spell was still on me.

"You've changed. You're different-looking, Matthew."

"Have I? A little heavier, that's all. But you . . . you're thinner, Eve. Have you changed?"

"I don't think I have. You said you'd write. Why didn't you?"

"I said I would. I did. I wrote a postcard. Things work out differently sometimes. I knew we'd meet sometime. Fate. I've put on a little weight admittedly."

My mood had quite changed, I was elated. The perfume bar girls were eyeing me. Mrs. Quest was watching. The face that kissed, that said sweet things, was near again. He'd picked me from a village dance, now he was picking me from a city shop, snug in a navy overcoat. I stepped from behind the counter, I looked at his soft moustache, brown with a slight curl, I looked at his rounder face, at his hair, longer now, and I smelled his dentisty breath. I walked on air, I didn't feel carpet under my feet as I left the perfumery. When my shoes were under the white tablecloth in the customers' restaurant, where the staff were forbidden, I remembered I'd not asked Mrs. Quest. My lap was touched by linen. He'd ordered lovely cakes, chocolate with cream swirls, whipped-cream ones with cherries, nuts. There was a soft napkin, China tea, tongs for lump sugar.

"Now, Eve, what have you been up to?"

"I thought you had forgotten, Matthew."

"Forgotten? As if I could. How long have you been in this part of our land? And are you here for good?"

And he became an obsession again, as he had been when I was in the country, waiting for a letter from him. I didn't think of Skin, I thought of Matthew. I waited every day, waiting for him to come to the perfumery. I never knew. He didn't arrange meetings.

He had explained to Mrs. Quest that I was an old friend, friend from the past, to please forgive him for abducting me so ungallantly. He'd like to buy something from her counter, what did she suggest? Mrs. Quest had looked at me, had smiled into the locked cupboard, opened it, smiled as she wrapped the gift and rang up thirty pounds. He'd gone. I had felt gilded. I had been kissed before the girls on the perfume bar, kissed twice, left to arrange soaps in a golden glow until closing time. I'd been unable to eat the rich cakes he had ordered. My heart and soul had feasted. He'd said he'd be seeing me, not to forget. I didn't know where he worked or lived, it didn't matter. He'd asked me to tea with him, in the customers' restaurant, had poured Earl Grey tea for me while his own lovely teeth nibbled a cake. The cake smell, the soap smell at the counter, merged into a golden sensation. I wished that he knew the hostel telephone number. I waited for a call at the perfumery, though Mrs. Quest forbade personal calls.

He'd left after a glance at his expensive watch, his round face with the soft moustache had looked at me. He'd come again, not to forget him.

I told Omega that an old flame had asked me to tea. She was understanding, hadn't pressed me about future meetings, guessing that I didn't know. She had nobody, never went out, had never had a boy, no kiss of any kind. I didn't tell that he had bought perfume. I hoped that he was keeping it for me, for another time.

Each day I arranged the locked case with slow care, waiting for his return, trying not to look up unless I was addressed, trying to appear offhand. "Be seeing you" could mean a week, a month, a year. The purchase was a sign, he knew I liked scent. His important work tied him, he worked late, at the mercy of patients in pain. In the customers' restaurant he'd spoken again of my specialness, a starriness, a light over the clouds, I was enchanting. He'd remembered the way I moved, now he was bowled over again. A little thinner, but it suited me. I ought to eat more, have a cake. He'd not been able to believe his eyes, there, serving perfume in crystal bottles from a locked cupboard instead of teaching children. Had I left teaching? "Be seeing you" and "Don't forget."

Omega wanted me to describe him. She listened without envy, fiddling with the warts on her fingers. She'd no one to be dulally over. I'd had two, not bad for a country girl. She hated being black, living in a city like London where blacks were on sufferance and opportunities for romance were few. She imagined that a dentist would make a good lover, it went with all that probing. They drilled people into states of painlessness, leaving them soothed and better. I couldn't imagine Matthew hurting anyone, he was so smooth, leaning his

139

round face toward a pain-filled jaw, smiling, pressing a soft finger to a sore gum, shining a small mirror, fixing suctions, flashing a metal scraper, having plugged the cheeks with some wadding. I could see it all. I thought constantly of his distinctive smell, a dryness, more of a powder smell, made specially, I expect, to suit his personality, some type of after-shave. I told Omega who'd not known love a little about Skin, but not about my home life. How to survive in the metropolis was our main concern. She too found it daunting.

I was inking the till roll when he came again. I heard his soft voice.

"Evie. Here I am. Coming?"

"Matthew. It's not closing. I don't see how I can."

"Leave that to me. Wipe your fingers clean. Er . . . madam. I have a request. Another bottle, please, the same again. In fact, make it two. And I'll take Eve off your hands a little early, that's if you've no objection."

Mrs. Quest smiled again, lending me surgical alcohol for my hands, telling me to wash well before I got my coat. She rang up the sale herself. Her rules were strict, she couldn't risk the jealousy of the girls on the perfume bar, favoring the Irish girl, just come. But Matthew had spent a lot, and I was a hard worker.

"What would you like, Eve? How about a film?"

"You're taking me out? I don't . . . Which film?"

"There's a French one I would enjoy. *Les Deux Cousines*. What do you think?"

"I'd like it."

I hated films in foreign languages, particularly French. I didn't want reminding of Bridie and cattiness. But I couldn't risk displeasing. I'd fall in with any plan. He'd wait outside, he said, until I got cleaned up. The soap smeared blue with ink. I combed my hair, wishing I'd brought makeup. My coat was warm, borrowed from Omega, but cheap, with an imitation fur collar. The green lining had got torn, was pinned with staples. It would have been nice to be dressed expensively.

The cinema, for members only, was in a residential area. He leafed into his wallet for the card, telling me to buy sweets, handing me a fiver. I didn't like to buy a big bar, not wanting to seem greedy. I still loved chocolate. I felt ill at ease about rustling the wrapper while the audience enjoyed the French. Matthew leaned forward, caught up in the plot, refusing sweets. When I had finished he handed me his handkerchief, his profession made him used to mopping. Tissues for spit, water for rinsing, a pat on the shoulder. I felt sure I'd enjoy being drilled by him. The film bored me, I watched his profile, his slightly popping eyes, his moustache a blur in the dimness. Once, during a funny part, he put his warm hand over my sticky one. The audience laughed often but I only felt the sensation of Matthew's large hand. Omega's awful coat was lumped into the small of my back. I wished for the film to end.

"Intriguing," he said afterward, not commenting further, not asking what I'd thought of it. He smiled a little as he held the shabby coat out for me. Had I no scarf? Outside it was bitter. The tree twigs were brittle as pencil tracings against the night sky. It started sleeting. Snow didn't stay long in the metropolis, it became sleet, hitting on the skin, worse than gravel. Matthew said that the spring would be a long cold one and put up his umbrella. I wished I was the girl he thought I was, the girl that he remembered, white-skirted, wearing white dancing shoes, loving and helping my mother, but I'd changed.

Night in the metropolis accentuated contrast, made things blacker or more bright. Buses glared redly in the street lights, shadows were ink black. Car horns and brakes were shriller and everyone rushed. At this moment Mrs. Carter was probably reading her cup in the peace of the showroom, alone and sorry, imagining more beasts, bird shapes, or a ring. Matthew put driving gloves on, having buttoned Omega's coat. I needed a protector, I needed fattening up. Being with him, plus the sweets in the cinema, made me feel sick. The hostel food was poor, thin stews, gray vegetables, gray tea from an urn. But he didn't suggest eating. Time for one drink, he said, before he took me home. The pub was a quiet one, near the cinema, green-carpeted, with members of the audience in it, discussing the film in clever English voices. He ordered brandy, which tasted of burned cake. I quite liked it. I wished I could talk like the rest, cleverly, with technical expressions. It was the first pub I had ever drunk in. In the car afterward he asked why was I quiet. My stomach ached, I wanted to get back to Omega, yet I wanted to stay. He was exciting, tying my stomach in tangles. When we rounded the corner of my street he saw the hostel dangling with underwear. He was incredulous. The clothes were laughable, ghost rags in the snow. I saw Omega's vest. Some pale bloomers had been there since I arrived.

"It's a tradition. They always did it. They think it is a joke, or lucky possibly."

Flags, posters, effigies, or an array of underwear, such things helped people to go on. He said he could imagine the stares of old men. It brightened the dull street, he granted that. He couldn't get over linking up with me. A store, of all places. How was I getting on?

"Not badly. I don't like it. I expect it takes some time."

Home and the village people were light-years away, yet it was the city I missed most. I missed the Carters. I dare not think of Skin. Here in the metropolis they were without kindness. The ones most prone to smiles were black. I was fortunate to have Omega. I would have liked to know Mrs. Quest, but here class mattered. She couldn't show favoritism, befriend one of her staff. Friends were allowed inside the hostel, I told Matthew. I wanted him to meet Omega, alone in the dayroom, watching President Kennedy on the television, the only love of her life. She leaned forward to peer, hair frizzing in a bush, not turning until Matthew sat by her, a wedge of her face looking around, her chin, the inner corners of her eyes, her nose and broad lips leather-colored inside the bushy mop. Sometimes she used hair-straightener.

"Eeeh. You must be Matthew. Eve told me. Cold weather, isn't it?" She picked at her warts, trying to be at ease.

"Why didn't she tell me about you? I can't think why not. You're beautiful, Omega. Why didn't you say you have a lovely friend, Eve?"

"I haven't had a chance. I wanted you to meet."

"Alone are you, Omega?"

She looked at her fingers, twisting them. "Eve told me you were a dentist. You like it?"

"A dentist? Do I like it? On the whole, yes. I'd say by and large I like it. One might as well enjoy the work one does."

"Eeeh. Do you prefer lady patients?"

"I make no distinction. It's my rule to approach each case individually."

He explained about the deftness needed for his work, the detailed intricacy of it. It often left him drained. He wished that he could see more of me. His work precluded it. It was quite arduous.

"*Eeeh*. You must be sensitive, Matthew. A bit of understanding is worth a lot. Eh, Eve?"

Omega glanced back at the President, waving a kind hand to the New York crowds, another sensitive person, and popular. The television was Omega's survival.

"Er . . . sensitivity is important, I agree, plus knowledge. The training is detailed and precise."

Omega sighed. He repeated that she was too beautiful to sit alone. I wondered if he'd say the same if he saw her thick body underneath her vest. To sit night after night in the dayroom on a dark green plastic chair, alone in the light from the television, was lowering to morale. Omega ate too many snacks.

"Where do you live in London? I came from Manchester once."

"The outskirts. A bit outside London, easy enough by car."

"Near your practice?"

"Quite near. Yes."

Omega sobbed for Manchester quite often. The metropolis had let her down too. She had expected a bright new life after running away from home and I was her first friend, though she had been here for years. I wished she looked more attractive. After a crying spell she looked a fright, puffier than the Duke of Windsor. Her nighttime tears tended to return at breakfast, dribbling onto her plate as she cried for something more satisfying. Matthew seemed to transfigure her. She looked dreamy, pretending perhaps that she was his patient, speechless and gagged under his hands, being made comfortable by those nice fingers, or being raised in his electrically operated chair before the drill buzzed. She wanted me to work at the factory with her. I wanted to stay with Mrs. Quest, where the pay was better than a factory. I wouldn't have met Matthew at a factory, I had my store to thank. Now, I used lipstick a little, rubbed to a blur, and a stick of blue eye shadow. It took time to become a metropolitan. Matthew said Omega had fine teeth inside her beautiful face. I walked into the hall to kiss him, to avoid embarrassing her. As he left her he touched her woolly hair lingeringly, making her feel precious. Again he said nothing about meeting me.

The following week it got suddenly much colder. I woke with my jaw aching. A tooth at the back throbbed. I looked over at Omega, a hunch under her blankets, stirring, sitting up. She wore a stocking cap to straighten her hair, which she had soaked in a solution, and the elastic cut into her forehead. She breathed quickly, stretching and groaning. When she understood that I was in agony she smiled. Now was the chance to test Matthew. Cheer up, the pain would soon get better. Ring Matthew. I told her I didn't know the number.

Mrs. Quest lent me a wool scarf for my neck. I was to take aspirin with my coffee. I was to stay in the stockroom, checking invoices. My swollen face was no advertisement for her products, wouldn't grace any counter. Ugly, red-nosed, and uncomfortable, I sorted a stack of papers, each to be stamped, recorded, filed. Life was a paper chase, people chasing each other with recorded messages, people waiting to be chased. It was so cold.

"Eve. Here is your friend again."

I jumped. He was like magic, here when he was needed, come to help me, come to give his skill.

"What is it, Evie mine? You're not well, is it your ear?"

"My tooth. I couldn't sleep. The cold." I tried to turn from him, to hide my ugliness, my swollen cheek, my uncurled greasy hair. He'd never seen me draggled.

"Come. I'll soon see to it. I will fix you up. Madam, I know you will excuse her and forgive."

Money changed hands again, another flacon for his pocket, more ringing for the till. He waited while I got my coat. Brandy, that's what I needed, brandy would work wonders. He had a flask in his glove compartment. Poor darling, I hadn't been looking after myself.

I relied totally on his ability. Matthew with his skill would take my tooth in hand, having first primed me with brandy. He would be kind when he probed my mouth. Kindness would cure. Mr. Killem, Mr. Canner, Mrs. Carter, the tender care of Skin, each in his own way kind, each leaving memories. This was new, an English kindness. The face you first kissed influenced you most. I could never forget Matthew's first kiss under the apple tree. Now, large, warm in his coat, he guided me to his car. Sealed in leathery privacy I would recover. He had pain killers at home. His flask was silver, leather-covered. I swallowed a little more.

"Then shall we go to your surgery? I want to see your electrical chair. I expect it's quite modern."

"Electrical chair?"

"Your dentist's chair. Your surgery. All your equipment."

"It's not a surgery. I'm taking you to my house."

"Oh. Is your practice in your house?"

"No. Not at home. Elsewhere."

"Where is it? Why won't you say?"

"I have no surgery, Eve."

"How can you work as a dentist?"

"I'm not a dentist. Not in the strictest sense."

"You don't fix teeth, or extract them?"

"Not real ones."

"Are you a quack, Matthew?"

"Good God. I'm certainly not. I am a mechanic."

"Mechanic? For teeth? Machinery to do with dentistry? Equipment, do you mean?"

"I work in the dental field. I work with teeth. I make them. I don't repair real ones, I manufacture them. Bridges, caps, crowns, dental replacements of all kinds. That is my field."

I had been cheated. I saw him differently. He wasn't a professional man, he was a technician. I felt cold and let down. My dental protector was a liar. I listened to him explaining that he could help. He didn't personally attend the mouth but he had influence. He could arrange appointments quickly. He supplied appliances for a group practice. He stressed the skill required, the long training, the aptitude essential for such a job. He kissed my good cheek softly, stroked me with a rounded hand. Let him end my discomfort, put me right. Understand, he worked with teeth, ones that looked very real. Also, he had quite a knack with pain. His eyes went rounder with his sincerity. He spoke again about technicians, how they were needed as much if not more than dentists.

"Does it take long to make a plate?"

He told me it depended. Color matching could be tricky, getting the lower and upper jaw to synchronize took time. Getting the bite right took patience. Patience and accuracy were paramount. A careless plaster impression could ruin the finished product. He took pride in a perfect bite.

"I only wish you had told me. I'd like to see you do them all the same. I'll have some more brandy, please."

I wondered hazily about his cupboards stacked with rows of cast-off dentures, row after row of artificial grins, shading from milk white to pale brown, with many-colored gums. Molds, polishing machines, broken plaster casts, were what he worked on, not real smiles inside real heads talking with real lips. I recognized the smell now, not after-shave made specially, but plaster dust that came from his work, the cold clean smell of plaster. He could have fixed my father's tooth, snapped by Maxie's fist. I'd not visited a dentist since leaving Mother Perpetua.

"We'll make arrangements. You could do with some crowning, I'd say offhand, a little overcrowded. Not that your mouth isn't a delight. Leave it to me."

I drank again from the silver flask, wondering about crowning. Crowns had jewels, did they put jewels in the mouth, a gilded, jeweled smile? Would I have gems? I'd sooner flowers. I felt blurred. Flowers, jewelry, would improve many faces. It was a pity he had lied.

"Little dreamer. How are you now? It could be just neuralgia."

He stressed the psychological aspect of tooth replacement. Age, reincarnation, the cult of wearing teeth for ornament, signaling victory. A tooth symbolized retention, grip on life. Losing them was a pity, he restored what had been lost.

He was glad I was imaginative, a thinking girl, taking an interest in people. Omega, poor kid, she couldn't help her color, but she was limited. Had I other friends? He'd help any friend of mine, in any way.

148

"I only know you."

"I'm more than a friend, Evie."

He said my name lingeringly. The parking lot was emptying. His hand touched under my clothes.

"Don't, Matthew."

All the same I felt glad that I had nice things now, under my dress. I bought flowery matching bra and pants sets with my wages each week, like other girls. Some saved for a trousseau. But I wouldn't marry, no wearing lace in a church or pushing prams. Omega and I agreed that life was a jigsaw, you adapted, made it fit to suit you. Since leaving Skin in the city I'd lost several pounds.

"Shy little flower, aren't you?"

"I've more experience of life than you might think. A bit more than you realize."

"You have? We'll go now back to my place."

"Why have you been so secretive, Matthew?"

"I thought . . . You haven't guessed, then?"

"Guessed what? You should have told me before, about your work."

"I'm married, Eve. I'm not free, not as free as I could wish."

He gave a gusty sigh over the steering wheel. My surprise was mixed with a surprising nausea. I'd not eaten all day. I might have to lower his window, smear up his Triumph with brandy-smelling sick. Fear of this happening was stronger than surprise at his news. He wasn't free. His car might be disgraced. I wasn't so surprised. Of course he was married. It explained things.

"You're not angry, are you, Eve?"

"Could you drive more slowly, please?"

"You're not furious?"

"No. I am not. Please, slower."

"Evie. I'm afraid it's been a shock to you. I would have told you. I was waiting to pick the moment."

"How long have you been married?"

It was sad that my dream of Matthew was broken. But he'd got me off work early, was making a fuss of me. Since meeting up with him again the days went quicker, wishing and wondering if he'd come. He was showing me life: foreign films, brandy, though it made me feel sick.

"Five, six months. I never got over you, Eve, you were in my system. Meeting you again has convinced me of it. I don't want it to make a difference. You understand, don't you? You forgive?"

"Forgive what?" I felt another surge in my stomach. I must not spoil the car.

"You're not bothered then, about my marriage?"

"I have been alone. Just Omega and me, no one to talk to. Then you came. I like it with you."

The trick to holding back vomit was to talk slowly, for him to drive slowly, to move and breathe slowly.

"That's how I hoped you'd be. My marriage is a modern one. You are my star, Eve, my certain star."

"All the same, you should have said. Is she a Londoner?"

"Yes."

He must have married soon after his one postcard to me. Or he might be lying, have been married for years. I wondered what his English wife was like, if she had Nordic eyes, smooth lemon hair, and pearl studs in her ears. She might be a Laura or a Helen, with a private education behind her, emancipated like him, her ring no hindrance to her freedom.

"Is she beautiful?"

"Yes. I was afraid that your faith, your background, would make you refuse to see me."

"I've no faith. I chose to forget those things, a long while back."

Sick, betrayed, I sat rigid. He was a Bluebeard. There might have been others besides Laura or Helen, one after another, stacked behind a bolted door.

We turned abruptly into a drive with two white gates. The house had Tudor beams. Rhododendrons bushed each side of the porch hung with a storm lantern. Sleet smattered in gusts onto the porch roof. The lantern swung on its chain. In spite of the storm the place seemed as lifeless as an old picture, gracious but dead. Laura or Helen had an impressive bargain. I forgot my tooth, forgot my brandy-tasting nausea, I wanted to see inside. He got his keys eagerly. I must hurry into the warmth, the cold wouldn't help my condition. I wondered if Laura or Helen was out with someone else.

Inside was warm, a warm feel on the cheeks. I smelled his powdery smell more strongly, also a flower smell. The door opened into a big hall with thick gray carpets. Central heat and gray curtains made it luxurious. There was a knight in armor, nearly as tall as myself. More carpet muffled the stairway with oak banisters. There was an oak chest and a coat of arms. The knight's closed visor had a sneaky expression, not unlike the schoolies'. Opposite the oak front door was an open fireplace. He lit a cigar, then lit the paper. Soon smoke was curling round the logs, making the sap hiss. He put out his foot to a flying spark. The hearth rug was pale fur. There wasn't a speck of dirt, clean as a picture, inside and out. The faint floweriness came from a jar of potpourri. Various doors opened off the hall, all closed. He said he preferred the hall when he was alone.

151

"It's . . . baronial. Those are apple logs, I recognize them. Your wife is out, then?"

Out at the opera, her lemon hair trailing across a mink collar, waving a Turkish cigarette into the eyes of her escort? Or eating seafood, clothed tightly in satin, her Nordic eyes indifferent?

"Of course she's out. She does film work. She . . . takes herself off. Small parts, walk-ons usually. I'm used to her going away. She likes it. Our life . . . suits us."

His round eyes had a special warmth when he spoke of her.

"This is your own house?"

"I bought it before I met my wife. We've settled very well."

He kicked a log, making more sparks. The cigar smell, the logs, the flower smell combined fragrantly. He'd finished explaining his domestic setup. Now, what about my coat? Relax, I must get warmed through. Comfy, I sat on the fur rug. I watched him get glasses. He said we might eat later, another drink now, and a real talk. He had some tincture upstairs for my tooth, drink first. The word "upstairs" had special meaning, he'd managed it casually. I sipped quickly. I wasn't the green girl he had thought, not stupid, ignorant of worldly ways. The man sitting on the settle by me was someone else's husband, looking admiringly. It wasn't husband snatching, it was experience. I wasn't snatching the dentally qualified husband from Laura or Helen but gathering more experience. His hand caressed my neck. My collarbone, my cheeks, my ears warmed. There, wasn't that nice? he whispered. He loved my brogue, my breathy voice, my skin. My teeth, though out of line, were starry. Go on, take off your shoes.

152

"I'd like to see . . . upstairs. You said you had some tincture?"

I wanted to see Laura or Helen's room before we went further. I pushed at his pushing hands. I must see Laura's bath. My nausea was gone. I must see Helen's bed. I felt the thick gray carpet ruffling my soles as he pushed and half carried me, eager to get me up. The stairs were so soft. I tripped halfway up, pulling us both down.

"Stay. Wait, Eve, wait a minute."

And he was kissing me. The fire made kissing sounds. I could see before I closed my eyes the top of the knight's visor through the oak banisters. I lay on Matthew's legs, my own legs sloping up, my feet above my head. Precariously positioned I depended on him, depending on his hold. This was how birds were, soaring between earth and cloud, safe and yet not safe. I longed to be dependent always, on somebody dependable, held in a rocking sensation while the fire hissed. And it was over. He shifted, his hands gripped my shoulder blades, pulling his knees up, pulling me up. My flowered pants, when we found them, were on top of the knight's visor. He reached down for them, rubbing navel and hairs, not to worry, there, not sticky. Comfy? I'd like to wash now, wouldn't I? We mustn't forget the tooth tincture either. How was the tooth? The bathroom there was the spare one, come to the one off the main bedroom, their room.

The bath was another picture, colored delicately. Huge, round, a light shade of lilac, with water that flowed from open beaks. I descended steps into the bath. The bird taps glared with metal eyes as I stepped into their water, the wrong lady in the wrong place. There was a bidet and soaps of many colors. I patted

153

the swansdown puff from the crystal bowl over my hip bones, tried various oils, before wrapping a warmed towel round me. I squatted on the bidet where Laura or Helen squatted, pulled paper from the roll her hands had pulled.

It was delightful to make myself comfortable in another's home. Delightful to sit on a round bed with another's man. Soon I'd be harder than ever Eileen had been. It was a vast bedroom, in gray and lilac, neat, warm, clean. When he opened a wall cupboard I saw his hobby. Electrical gadgetry of all kinds. He liked to tape sounds, voices, tinkering with sounds. He wanted to tape my voice, so sweet, my breathy brogue would sound sweet in his ears after I'd gone. Would I? Had I found the tincture, made myself comfy?

"Why do you want my voice? I've never done it."

"You will love it. Your brogue is delicious, really."

"I don't know what to say."

"Read something. Here."

I flipped the pages of the poetry book written by James Stephens, feeling uncomfortable. Hadn't Skin said I must be my own conscience? I found one that I knew. "I am searching everywhere, but I cannot find the place."

"Why should you care, Eve? It takes two to go wrong. If his wife leaves him, why should you worry?"

"He can do as he pleases, I know. But sometimes I feel . . . bad."

"Don't, Eve. Did he say anything about me afterward?"

Omega was livelier since Matthew had come into our lives. She hardly cried at night, but plied me with questions, her black eyes sparkling. In touching her hair and complimenting her, Matthew had made her feel included.

"He's not free, Omega. Supposing I cause harm to them?"

Supposing I harmed myself. Often I felt jealous, hating Laura or Helen, wishing her dead. Sometimes I wished myself dead, wished to be someone different. It was then that I didn't admire Matthew, I despised him. I was enslaved.

"Cause harm then. All is fair in the love game. You're not his first, I'll bet you're not the last. All of the gents play games."

Omega had no experience other than the family she'd run from in Manchester, and what she overheard in the hostel. Conclusions were bitter. Love wasn't smooth anywhere. She'd have Matthew if I'd finished with him, be next in his line. She'd been concerned that night, about my tooth, had waited with milk in a thermos, had drawn conclusions when I'd not come in. How was the tooth anyway?

"I forgot about it."

"Did he see to it before or afterward? *Eeeh*. Fancy on the stairs."

"He isn't a dentist, Omega."

"*Eeeh,* what a lying Arab. He said he was."

She'd gone to pains, straightening her hair since meeting him. The Arab. It only showed, if you got involved, you got let down. President Kennedy wouldn't do that, he was safe. What did Matthew do for work?

"He makes crowns, the kinds of teeth that you screw in. He makes and repairs false ones. I ought to stop seeing him."

"Well, you got some nookies. You had a nice time. *Eeeh*, Eve, don't drop him."

Omega spoke of nookies with longing and curiosity. She blamed her color and her warty fingers for the lack of romance in her life. We both had tried to slough our old skins off, snaking to new experience. Often I felt that Matthew was an anxiety rather than a pleasure. His Laura or Helen ruled our meetings, depending on her rehearsing or auditioning, leaving the house empty. I'd stopped eating sweets. I wanted a new coat to meet him in. Omega said I should ask. Grab cash from the Arab. Grab some of the green scent too. He'd money, hadn't he? A smart home, two cars, and a wife away often. What was keeping me? When were we meeting next?

"I don't know. I never know."

"Be firm. Assert yourself, Eve."

156

I hadn't told that he'd left me at my job the next morning without giving me breakfast, rushing away to his technician work. Earlier, before we left Slough, I'd heard him on the telephone by his round bath, softly talking. I guessed that it was Laura or Helen, engaging him, on his mind still. I'd seen him look in his letter-box. Looking for a letter from her? In villages, cities, and here in the metropolis it was the same, emotional security sought from pieces of paper slipping into a letterbox. He'd forgotten to ask about my tooth, dressing hurriedly, waiting while I combed my hair, impatient to get me away. He'd slept deeply, ignoring me by his side. He'd muttered once, a name like Jane, not Laura or Helen. Matthew and Jane. It sounded right. I was afraid of seeing him again. I was dying for it.

And three days later he appeared, tapping the show-case with rounded fingers, ordering another bottle, wafing me away again, having placated Mrs. Quest. How about another French film? Or should we go straight back to Slough? He didn't suggest a meal. I'd had no food with him, apart from the cakes the first time, which I'd been too excited to eat. I think he was ashamed of my coat. He drove fast, his left hand on my thigh. The weather was still dreadful.

"How long will your wife be away this time?"

"Probably the rest of the week."

"You miss her, don't you?"

"I never said I didn't. Our way of living is unusual, I suppose."

"You're close to each other basically. You love her."

"We are bound. Marriage isn't roses. Even you, Eve, wouldn't imagine that, would you? Separation, change, keeps the bond fresh. Are you quite comfy?"

"And me? Where do I fit in?"

"I told you, Evie innocent, you are my colleen. I wouldn't like to lose you."

"You have had many girls, before me?"

Had there been a Jane in his past, a Jane he still dreamt of, or was it his wife?

"Girls? What girls? You are my only girl. I never forgot about you, after that Irish holiday."

"Why did you marry?"

"The stability. She needs me. My wife . . . I couldn't imagine life without her."

"Where did you meet each other?"

"The Café de Paris actually. Superb. She's a superb dancer. She's always wanted to act. She takes elocution and dancing lessons."

"I don't understand you, Matthew."

"Don't try, my innocent. My wife needs what I give her. Enjoy life. My wife is . . . She's my wife. You are my certain star."

"What is she like?"

I had to know. Once started I couldn't stop, like probing a painful tooth, testing for pain. There were no photographs in the Slough home, nothing to give me a clue. I had to find out. What did she look like? And had there been more like me, temporary, expendable? Was he a secret Bluebeard? He took out a snap from his wallet.

"She is from Scotland, though you'd not tell from her speech."

"So this is her, is it?"

"You can't see her very well. It was our honeymoon actually." He explained that she had moved, had been unwilling to pose because he had wanted to include the mountain behind her. She liked the limelight, rightly so, preferring close-ups.

The girl on the grassy slope could have been Julie Andrews or Mrs. Gandhi. Hair over her face, knee deep in flowers, she could be anyone. The mountain peaks, the spires of the Swiss village, were sharply clear. Laura or Helen or Jane, a smudge in the foreground was still an enigma, still an object of jealous inquiry. She had the blurred outline of a successful poacher, rather windblown.

"I can't tell if she's beautiful. Blond, is she?"

"She changes. She is beautiful, believe me. Can you see me involved with anyone plain or ugly? I love beauty, Evie. Beauty like yours."

He couldn't help boasting. His house, his car, his gadgetry, the beauty of his wife. Now that I understood that his work was more than just getting the bite right, he boasted of the speed with which he turned out dentures. He was a superstar. He believed his wife had star qualities. And me, I was his certain star. What luck that I'd come into his life again. His wife, that first time he'd discovered her at the Café de Paris, had colored her hair a shade called pink galaxy. He would do anything for her. And me too, of course, waving his hand in an expressive way, the hand with the gold ring set with a diamond.

"What do you wish most for, Matthew, most in the world?"

"More money and more women. A dozen, with you the favorite." I was so open, so constant, so receptive. I deserved the best.

He touched me again. The hand lifting my clothes was wearing gold. When I felt him I forgot Laura or Helen or Jane, forgot everyone but us. I forgot to feel threatened by the one who owned him, owned his support, his first allegiance.

When he went into his bathroom I opened one of the wall cupboards, quietly. Arranged on plastic heads, with eyelashes and gaping mouths, was an array of wigs, all colors. I shut the door quickly. I'd already looked in the bathroom cupboards, over the round basin with the bird taps, had seen the supply of bottles multiplying in the mirror behind them, ensuring that the face they painted would be a secure investment, a stepping-stone to stardom. She had a sports car. He told me that sometimes she only came home to change, make a few telephone calls, and fill her car with fresh accessories before leaving again. His smile was special and loving when he mentioned her, his only wife. Her self-centered grasping face kept him captivated.

"Now then, my innocent, my Evie, here is your drink. Kiss me."

The round bed was a familiar place now, I and the lilac sheets were old friends. I understood the various switches, aids to comfort. I'd never go near the cupboards again, or tell him about my family. He asked me nothing, occupied exclusively with his own affairs. I was valuable, I was unselfish, his treasured star to be petted and made comfy. With his hands on me I forgot everything but present pleasure, learning, absorbing. He taught me to explore, to enjoy the unusual, to love experimentally. Unusual places, moving unusually in unusual pleasure, was a technique, he'd even call it a craft. In the big round bath, filled with scented water for our pleasure underneath the shower. Across the bidet under the glaring birds' eyes. Behind the window curtains, wrapped in velvet. He liked to record sounds of love, it interested him.

Thanks to his teaching I was superb. He took credit for performances, I was a source of pride. He'd admitted that he'd like to be a sex therapist. Either that, or run an agency for "hostesses." He felt he had a calling in this field, to give advice or help in sex problems. There was a need, the world waited to be shown the more refined pleasures of the flesh. He had the key to satisfy demand, Alas, the mortgage, providing for his wife's needs, were pressures he could not ignore. He had to keep his steady dental job, sex therapy must remain a dream for the time being. Granted teeth were important, but sexual congress was vital. He was absorbed in the supplying of a man's needs, inventing fresh ideas, experimenting. At the risk of sounding immodest, he wouldn't mind staging demonstrations. A big stage, nothing hole-and-corner, nothing shabby, but something suave, expensive, for club members. He had the expertise, he'd wait. Meanwhile he had me.

After a few more visits there wasn't a nook or cranny of his picture-book house in Slough that hadn't been made use of. This way and that, no end to invention. Over the hood of his car in the warm garage, on top of the freezer, buttocks getting chilled. Up in the attic, next to the hot water tank. He'd only to put his gold-beringed hand out in a special way and I'd be compliant, supple, willing. I thought less and less of Laura or Helen away at her acting or standing on mountains with hair blown over her face. He was left free and available. I was the stealthy poacher now, and liking it. Omega was right, men played games. Games that I'd not give up for the silly reason of a marriage. Each time when I got back, Omega was waiting, questions in her black eyes. Questioning me about the nookies, had it been nice? I told her everything. My dancing experience stood me in good stead, I was more agile than a snake.

I found the bottles bought from the store, unopened, piling up, all bought for his wife, ignored and unappreciated. He'd never bought me anything, aside from the one chocolate bar in the cinema. He never gave me food. I was his sex toy. I would have liked some of the scents that his wife's spoiled fingers hadn't bothered to unwrap, some little gift. His vaunted salary was kept for her.

"Assert yourself, Eve. Get something. I'd love to be asked there. I'd make sure of something."

"I'll ask if you can come, Omega. A little party. Matthew would probably like the idea."

I suggested it to him. Poor Omega had no one and nowhere to go. She so hated being black and wanted so much to be like an ordinary English girl.

"Poor beauty. I'll pick up the two of you. Next time. Soon, very likely."

He hurried to his job. He never made me late for work. His face had a faraway look, the planning of a new thrill. Three, one black, one white, and him. He'd tape it in stereo, stage it all nicely. He'd try to let me know beforehand.

"It's arranged then, Omega. Slough. You can come nest time."

"*Eeeh.* Nookies? Did he say when? I'll buy a sexy outfit."

"He never knows. He'll come, he always does."

"I'll buy something in limey yellow."

She pinched at her warts. She asked me to go with her to choose.

We went to the shop where she'd bought the awful coat that I wore, near the chip shop on the corner. Our street and the streets round it smelled of grease, even in this weather. Grease and the sad coldness of dirty snow.

The dress shop was dispiriting, with the same window display that never changed, containing sleazy clothes which Omega thought beautiful. A newspaper had blown against an empty bottle crate in the doorway, frost-rimed, wrapped stiff against the corners. Three unwashed milk bottles were rimed with a ridge of white.

Inside was the same grease smell. It wasn't warmer in the empty shop. There were no customers. The assistant studied her nails, not looking up. She was black too, but not as black as Omega. She had no interest in the supply of limey yellow two-pieces. On Omega's insistence she climbed in the sleazy window to undress the plaster model. Faded over the bosom, its seams cracking as Omega forced her body in, it was the two-piece of her dreams. The shoulders strained out of alignment, the zipper split. Lovely, wasn't it? She turned before the dirty mirror. Exactly what she wanted, a good fit too, really. She'd have to fight the gents off. She would pay weekly, there'd be no discount even though the front was faded, it was that kind of shop, used by the underpaid and underprivileged. Omega would buy a plum-colored lipstick, shave under her arms a bit. Her hair would be straighter than horsehair for the great night out. She wished she could manage shoes, regretted the money she'd frittered away on snacks. The assistant wrote in an old book, unsmilingly, her expression unchanging throughout the transaction, used to overhearing the hopes and excitements of dates, the wax and the wane of romance.

Out in the road again was a chimney sweep, a lucky omen for Omega. "Acme will clean your flue," the van said. Blackness wasn't necessarily a bad condition, if you had the power to remove it, or to place it where it was welcome, it was sad that Omega hadn't a choice.

163

The man winked. If a sweep kissed a bride the marriage prospered.

"*Eeeh.* I'll never marry, Eve. Who do I meet?"

This time Matthew telephoned the store, made the arrangements. He'd come on Saturday.

Omega was ready early, waiting in the dayroom wearing her limey yellow, indifferent to television today. Now she was equal, or almost equal, to the other girls, a gent was coming for her, a gent she was to share, but still, a gent. She'd bathed, she'd shaved, she worked upon her warts, making them bleed a little, but her hands were smooth, the pink inner surfaces delicate. Her hair was stiff from the straightener. She got into the front of Matthew's car without hesitation, turning her face from one window to the other, black queen of the world. Matthew drove fast.

"What is the program? Drinkies first, before Slough? Shall we be stopping?"

"Plenty of time later for drinks, Omega," he answered, accelerating.

Her two-piece dress seemed to quite shock him, also her strange lime smell, oil bought from an Indian. She was a different Omega from the lonely cast-down girl he'd seen first. It took some adjustment. He said it was too cold, leaning away from her, narrowing his round eyes.

Omega craned her short neck as we turned into his white gates. *Eeeh.* He had lit the log fire earlier, a welcome all in readiness. We stood round it, snow-smattered, watching the flames. Omega opened her short coat of imitation fur, showing the limey yellow in its full glory.

"*Eeeh,* what's the nice smell?"

"Potpourri. And the apple logs," I said.

164

I was the hostess now, displaying the home's attractions, revealing my territory to Omega. Matthew's cigars, the fire, the potpourri smell were heady. Omega peered into the porcelain jar. What flower petals had they dried to smell so nice? She looked at the knight's visor. What was inside him? *Eeeh*, he must have seen some sights. She kneeled to stroke the fur of the hearth rug, what animal was it? She loved everything, all nicer than I'd led her to expect. She crawled across the carpet, touching the wood settle, what wood was it? And the kitchen? A modern one, she'd bet. *Eeeh*. Matthew smiled tightly. He asked if I'd do the honors, serve drinks from the oak corner cupboard. He heaped more logs on, puffing his cigar in a cloud.

"Rum, please, Eve," she said, her black eyes gleaming. Rum was the drink of her people, back in Manchester when they'd been together. Rum gave you heart, rum made it a party.

After three glasses she started giggling, the mirth flowing down her cheeks in a wet stream, worse than my mother. Mirth dripped onto the limey yellow of the cloth stretched over her bust. A lock of her straight hair disengaged from the rest in a black spike. Another? She'd not say no. What about a ciggy from that nice box? *Eeeh,* Turkish.

"Comfy then?"

Matthew told me to find some cocktail biscuits, mustn't let Omega go overboard, not too early. I saw him noticing the feet of her tights, shredded from wearing at work, from making corn plasters. The shop allowed only so much credit, the two-piece outfit was all they'd allowed her. She burst into another fit of laughing. Every girl deserved a place like this, no matter

165

what her color or her work. Another one or two rums and she'd be ready to inspect the big round bed.

"Plenty of time. Have a biscuit."

Matthew poured brandy for himself and me, his eyes going up the ladder on Omega's thigh. I puffed nervously on a cigarette. I supposed he'd had experience handling new girls, girls like Omega, awkward and inexperienced. I'd never seen her like this.

"Whoops. *Eeeh*, mustn't spoil the nice rug."

She sank down over the spreading liquid. More spikes of her hair stuck out from the rest, she picked at the bits of broken glass in the hearth. Matthew picked up the siphon. Enough was enough. Bed was the place for passing out. Upstairs now, Omega. He tugged at her limey skirt, the hem already hanging down. He bit his teeth into his cigar. Up, Omega. His glowing cigar end touched a black spike, making a bad smell and a fizz. Upstairs, no more drinking, enough was enough.

I pulled the pink palms upraised on the rug. Once upright she could just walk, supported on either side. She giggled as she hit the newel post, pausing on every step. Which part, Eve? Where on the stairs had I had nookies? Here, stretched at an angle? *Eeeh*. Where was the toilet? Quick. Matthew grimaced. He threw his cigar over the banister, into the hearth. We had to push Omega across the corridor. Omega, easy, clothes down first. There. Come out when you're ready. Matthew and I will wait. There was a silence. After a while we heard taps running, Omega was using the birds' beaks. She wasn't at all suitable, we'd started off wrongly. I didn't know if I should go to her, explain to her about dignity. The door opened. Her lime knickers were still down, encumbering her large knees. She'd washed. She

166

was still giggling. *Eeeh,* round bath, round basin, round bed. Was it a water bed? She fell on it.

"Not on the bedspread. Up, beautiful. Just a minute, bedspread off first. To be more comfy."

Matthew eased the quilt, folding it down neatly. Omega settled on the eiderdown. Matthew removed his shoes of best pigskin suede and then his trousers. He folded them with care, getting the creases right, his stomach under his underpants looking childish, familiar. Omega had curled into a ball, murmuring with pleasure. Matthew told me to undress, curtly, get on with the business, tugging at Omega's green knickers as he spoke. He looked revolted at having to touch either of us, much less at having an orgy. He wiped his forehead with his plump wrist. I pulled at my blouse miserably. I tried to shift Omega. Even a sweep wouldn't look at her now. Matthew got another cigar from the drawer. If he let her rest she might come around, be willing and eager for the multicolored orgy. A job once started must be finished. I wished that he was a proper dentist, used to more control, used to contrariness of people. Omega wouldn't roll over; she appeared to have stopped breathing. Move, Omega. Omega, please, come back to reality, we have come here for a purpose, don't you remember? Straighten out. I managed to get her onto her back. It was such a waste. She had prepared carefully. Grains of talcum lay in her groin, clung to her body hairs.

"Omega, move."

"Nookies. Who's for nookies?

"We'll have to wait, Matthew."

"Who's in charge of the proceedings, anyway?"

He looked enraged. A professional, he'd never failed, him with his expertise. And by Omega, who was muttering about Arabs now. He'd never been made to look so foolish. He went to the cupboard for his tape recorder. The evening was off to a poor start, doomed probably; still, he would record the sound of it as he always did. I wondered if he expected Omega to read "The Snare" by James Stephens after her initiation. Plump and cross in his underpants, he switched it on. I heard a voice, a humming sound, small, breathier than a whisper. *"Mais oui, madame. Mais oui, madame, que vous avez un beau bébé."* He pressed the switch.

"Wait, Matthew. Let me listen."

"I want to turn the tape over."

"Play that back, please. Switch it back, please."

I grabbed his hand, I had to listen. I heard the hum again, then the voice speak, quiet, a voice talking to itself. "It's about time that sweet cousin and I met up again. Long time no see. Her rendering of the poem was touching. Same old game, it never fails. She's sleuthed me long enough. Running in my footsteps in Ireland, calling me hard. The nerve, she's no innocent, here in my own home, following me. I've finished with her and that rotten childhood, I've got my razzle-dazzle. She'll be sorry. My own husband. Nerve. Rotten childhood, rotten country, rotten relatives. I'll make her sweat."

"That's just my wife. She practices her elocution. She uses the recorder, reading parts."

"Nookies. Have we done it?"

"She wasn't reading. That was her talking. She was talking about me."

"Nookies. *Eeeh.*"

"How could she know you? It was a part."

"She knows me, Matthew. That was my own cousin."

"It was Elaine. Elaine, my wife, rehearsing."

"Nookies, not a cousin."

"It was Eileen. My cousin from Ireland."

"Elaine was from Scotland originally. In her childhood. She's no Irish miss."

"What are you on about? Nookies."

"Eileen is my cousin. We were reared together."

"Elaine used the tape recorder, she was home last night."

"Will you please get on with nookies."

"We must go home now, Matthew. Come, Omega. Home now."

"You're both welcome to leave. My house is becoming a madhouse. I need another brandy. That was my wife."

"Me too. *Eeeh*."

"We have to go. Please."

He'd lost face. He'd been foiled by his own machine. His wife had the last say. No comfy orgy but defeat. My dental man had lost. What he had planned so confidently had flopped. Elaine had insinuated herself into the party and Omega had been too much to bear. Some girls weren't worth the effort. Yes, right, he'd take us now, with joy.

Eileen's sheets, the sheets of my own cousin, had felt the last of me. My feet touched Eileen's soft rug for the last time. Fur or soft leather, animals were useful alive or dead, after the trap got them. I longed to be a bird, without regrets, human feelings, or frailties. Eileen had caught me after I'd stopped chasing. I must get Omega away with what dignity I could manage, get the bearlike animal away from Slough. Metropolis people were the most cruel, indifferent to anyone's feelings.

Another drive into the black cold instead of fun in

lilac sheets. Matthew would replace me, adding to his fund of expertise, he wouldn't care. Elaine was happy, that mattered most to him. Sprawled and inert on the back seat Omega slept, her imitation-fur jacket covering her face. She groaned from time to time. The cold was piercing after the warmth of the lilac bedroom. He didn't bother to switch on the car heater for us. What did heat matter, he'd get back with all speed, to some peace and another brandy. To plan and seek out another partner. The world was full of girls waiting for his initiation. My last memory of Slough was the head of the visored knight, triumphant. Out with the poachers, stay on guard. The street lights shone on Omega, her spikes of hair, her dreadful tights. Matthew said nothing, his cigar an angry stump in his full lips. He drove fast, heedlessly braking round sharp corners, driving onto the pavement by the dress shop where the bottle crate was. He jerked to a stop near the dangling underclothes, stiff-dried, frozen. He hated touching, he used a pigskin shoe to help unburden his car of her, nor would she uncurl. She groaned again as she hit the pavement, settling again to sleep. He didn't wait, he'd delivered the goods, let me do the rest. It had been my idea. He didn't speak or turn back.

Oh, Omega, you big, drunk bear, get up. What have you done to me? I'm shamed, I'm cold, and I am disillusioned. Omega, you are too much for one person, move.

I left her there and went up to the door to ring, to get help from a cockney because Omega was too much. Sniggering, sneering, a girl came, helped her in. We undressed her, got her into bed while Matthew my first love sped back to his home. I'd never see Slough again,

170

I'd never see Eileen. Escaped and truly gone, she was a memory.

In the morning came a letter with a city postmark. I ripped it open quickly, my first news from Mrs. Carter. My financey had spoke. She'd went. He'd spoke two words to her. Travel home. He needed me. Fond friend, Mrs. Carter. The letter came at the right moment. I'd got all I could from the metropolis. I'd traveled, learned of the world's ways, earned my keep at the perfumery. Mrs. Quest had been kind. Omega, my one friend, would regret me. Matthew had taught me the mistake of trusting without knowing, the perils of indulgence without love. Racked, crazed, but I hadn't loved. I would go back over the water. My two city friends, Skin and Mrs. Carter, needed me. I told Omega the metropolis was too big, too sad, not right, I'd had enough.

"If I had a real cousin you'd not hear me complaining. Stay, Eve. See your cousin. Why should it matter? You never told me about her."

Omega couldn't understand. She'd heard no one speak in the lilac bedroom. What was wrong with me? Eileen might be pining for me for all we knew, what did it matter that she'd married my dental gent, all was fair in the love game. See Eileen. I might as well forget Matthew who'd dumped her in the street and probably doped her, nor did she remember any nookies. Bad Arab. But see Eileen.

"She made a fool of me. Matthew made use of me. I can see sense now."

"Forget him, duck. You used to be dulally, now you're not. Stay. Get another gent."

We both needed a couple of gents to buy green perfume for us, good hot food, some good coats, some more rum.

"It's . . . degrading. I hate it here now."

Different for Omega, who was resigned to her life in the metropolis. I wanted to put the open sea between me and Slough. Good riddance to that gray carpeting, that round bed and big bath, the knight and apple fire. Forget the hostel slung with ladies' bras, streets smelling

172

of grease, dirty snowdrifts, and those great red buses. Fly from the cold tight metropolitan faces and gloved hands of customers handing out notes at the perfumery. Pretend Matthew had never existed.

"I'd give a lot for someone to love, someone to be dulally over. Sometimes I miss my Dad. Why didn't you tell me, Eve? About your cousin?"

"I wanted to start fresh. Like you, Omega. I have an aunt here, somewhere. I don't remember her."

"See her, Eve. Your cousin's mother? Forget that cousin business, but see Auntie. She'll give you a nice tea very likely."

Omega would do anything. A welcome from my Aunty might make me change my mind, stay with her in the metropolis.

"I don't know her at all. Eileen lived all of her life with us in the country. Aunt never came."

"She never saw her daughter? Poor lady. See Aunty, I'll come with you."

It would be a good end to my travels to meet the aunt who had put Eileen from her, help lay the ghost of the girl, an exorcism. Eileen had found her Lord Right and razzle-dazzle. Neither was right for me. My last trip in this place would be to the sender of cards. "Hope all is well. Comps of the season." We'd go. Only Omega would miss me when I left. Mrs. Quest would have to train another girl for the perfumery, trusted keeper of the locked showcase. Omega would get another roommate. Our last Sunday jaunt would be to see Aunt.

"Where does she lives, Eve?"

"Near Stepney. I'll find the address."

I wrote a note to her. I heard nothing. I explained to Omega about my mother's old closeness with her sister, how marriage, birth of children, changed things. I wrote to Mrs. Carter, telling her to expect me. I had my ticket bought. Soon I'd be back with them, I'd see the whispering schoolies, discover if Biddy had been boiled, or was giving her egg a day.

"Why don't you go back to your real home? Your Mum and Dad are alive, back in that village. Don't they miss you?"

"Not now, not for a long time. I'm grown. I've friends in the city, and a boy I used to . . . I used to love. He got ill, nearly died."

"You're secretive. Dulally over someone else? *Eeeh,* Eve."

"I'm glad I've seen England. I've met you. I've had enough."

It was nice that the Carters wanted me. I had much in my favor. The schoolies might have more respect, now that I'd traveled. I'd go back to cleaning until Skin was better. My return would complete his cure. I might go back to the church of the novenas, light candles of thanksgiving to the Sacred Heart. That angry face would smile. I'd had enough of hurt. I longed to wipe ashtrays again, after the phoning was done. I'd have my cup read, Mrs. Carter would see flowers, bells for me and stars. The quare-shaped beasts were gone. Skin would be well, teach me about birds, gulls and nightbirds, the legendary ones, the phoenix and the roc. I'd finished with harpies and shock.

Omega put on the lime two-piece again for the trip to Aunt's. Knowing me had changed her, she'd cry no more tears, tears were destructive. She wanted to be more proud, proud of her black body, proud of her woolly hair. She'd stop gobbling snacks, mix more with her own kind. Self-confidence was catching, folk took

174

you at your own valuation. *Eeeh,* but she'd miss me. A shame about the dental gent, those in the dental trade must be a rum lot. She wouldn't fancy it herself, peering into one dirty mouth after another, making replacement parts. They had their place but she'd sooner her job in the factory, making foot medications, products for those with foot ailments. She thought I'd have been happier there than in the perfumery. Hers was interesting employment, the corn and toe powder section was lively, with a few other blacks and nobody to bully them. No need to leave because of a gent, join her on the corn plasters. I told her that Mrs. Quest had told me I ought to study, that I'd the ability. There was my city friend as well who'd been ill, wanted me. Omega said *Eeeh,* what about chiropody?

The girls on the perfume bar were glad. They had been jealous.

"Let's just hope Auntie will be in, Eve."

We went by tube. Omega wore a lime wool cap, pushed skyward by her springing hair. There was nothing about the metropolis I liked except the underground. To dive below the ground, to arrive within minutes at your destination, emerging like a burrowing animal, was the best form of travel. We thought the uncleanliness a pity. Rude signs on uncleaned wall tiles, dirt under your feet spoiled it. The magic of quick travel charmed me. I liked the escalators. I would tell Skin about these things. About the noise, the rattle, about the people's faces avoiding each other's eyes, about the hot thick stuffy smell. Omega said the suicide rate was higher underground. People reached depths of the spirit down there, flinging themselves on the electric lines, to be scraped later from the engine wheels. The train drivers got a fortnight off, official compensation

175

for accidental mishap, to get over their shock. I would remember the roar of the trains approaching, the stuffiness warming the stale air. There was no waste of time. We looked at underwear advertisements, more daring on the escalator than those out in the daylight, different from the drooping bits on the hostel windowsills.

Omega smoothed her crumpled skirt. She'd stitched the hem. She got out a Park Drive cigarette. Have one. Don't look at that sick pigeon at the end of the car, all loose wing feathers and misery. Birds shouldn't go in trains. The stickiness along its breast made it half dead-looking. Do not look. Ill luck to look at a dying bird, a bird here could mean death or violence. *Eeeh,* luckily I'd her to protect me. If Auntie turned out to be rude or vicious, she was there. Do not look at that pigeon. She picked lightly at her warts. She blamed work for them, toxic substances in the foot powders affected her poor fingers. She had tried many cures. She turned from the sick pigeon, puffing her Park Drive. She was dying to see Auntie. Up the moving stairs. *Eeeh,* look at the knickers, she'd not mind modeling ones like that. They didn't use black girls much, though. Was this Stepney? What a lot of blacks, she'd not mind living here. The newspaper man stared at her limey bust while giving directions to Aunt's street.

It was a narrow street, dirty and unswept, like most of them. Thousands of dirty and unswept pavements were all over the metropolis, thousands of row houses, thousands needing paint, needing clean curtains, needing some happier occupants, streets that stretched on forever. Aunt's house was near a prison. Forget ill birds and bad times, said Omega, think about Auntie waiting, making us tea. *Eeeh,* she was glad she had come. There, that was the house, the one with the worst windows and worst paint, that was Auntie's residence. We'd probably both love her, dear little Irish lady.

Her bell made a thick croak. We waited. I heard a police siren nearby. After the third croak of the bell we heard shuffling feet inside. The door opened a crack, still on the chain. A pinched face showed, years older than my mother's. Her jaw was square, like Eileen's had been, her eyes were sunken, with eyeblack sooted into the wrinkles, and thickly blackened brows. She looked incuriously at us, her pupils dull under short henna'd bangs. The rest of her hair was long, red, unsuitably styled. The door stayed at a crack. I stared back.

"Auntie. Hulloa, Auntie. I'm Omega. I've come along with Eve. I've kept her company because she's rather shy."

"I am Eve Joyne. I'm your niece. I wrote. Did you not get my letter? I am your Eileen's cousin."

"What's it?"

"Your sister is my mother. Where Eileen lived. In Ireland, remember? I'm going back next week."

"I'm Eve's best friend, Omega Tanner. Ome for short. I told her she should write. I made her come."

Omega spoke louder, thinking she might be deaf. Aunt didn't look at her, she only looked at me, staring with dull eyes. Omega pushed warty fingers against the door jamb. Aunt started to push the door closed.

"I'm leaving to go back. I had to see you first."

"What's it? Back?"

"To Ireland. Back to the city. I work there. I've friends in the city. You didn't mind me coming?"

"What's it? You ought to have writ first."

"*Eeeh,* you didn't get it? Shame. I posted it myself. I'm Eve's friend. Shall we come in, Auntie?"

177

She undid the chain, opening the crack a few inches, ignoring Omega.

"Wait for me, Auntie. I've come with Eve."

Omega was used to rudeness. She was amazed by Aunt, she wouldn't miss a minute of the meeting. She liked Stepney. Anyone so old, so bony and downcast, ought to be in nursing care. Her old black dress was crumpled. And that hair, white at the roots now that we saw her back. She should be in a home. Those collar and hip bones were shocking, the powder on her face flaked. Auntie needed a wash.

Inside was a dark passage smelling of cats. There was an umbrella stand with a long gent's umbrella.

"Nice little place, Auntie."

"Have you some message for anyone when I go back, Aunt?"

"What's it? Stay away."

"That's right, Auntie, that's what I tell her. Stay here. I can get work for Eve, work in the corn plasters. We could live here, to be near you. I like Stepney."

"I did work here. A perfume-selling job. I've left it. I've heard of Eileen. She is doing . . . well."

"What's it?"

"In films. Eileen gets work in films sometimes. She . . . married. Did you know?"

"Your daughter is kind of a film star, Auntie. Lives in Slough. *Eeeh,* but I'm thirsty after that journey."

Omega looked at Aunt's kettle, blacked with greased rust. Her scullery was narrower than Skin's kitchen. The table flap had to be lowered to reach the stove.

"I haven't seen Eileen. I . . . I have heard her speak. We were close once. We were brought up closely."

"What's it? Why've you come?"

178

"Eve told me you left your Eileen. My Mam used to threaten that. *Eeeh*. I left her. My thirst is massive. Blood counts in the end."

Aunt didn't glance at Omega or acknowledge her presence. Like an old sentinel bird she stood beside her stove.

"I'm sorry we're unwelcome. We'd best go, Ome."

"Films, eh? Done all right, did she? My girl done right for herself?"

"Done very well indeed, Auntie. Got hooked to a dental gent."

"What's this your name is?"

"Eve."

"I'm Ome."

"Don't you go back, Eve. Not back to that place. Bad country."

"I'm going to the city, Aunt. Not to the country. I'll write to my mother, say I've seen you."

"Go on, tell her to stay here, Auntie. *Eeeh,* I'll miss Eve."

"Do you want a cup, Eve?"

"If it's no trouble, Aunt. We both would."

I wondered if Aunt had had a stroke, or was born backward.

"I'm parched, Auntie. I like your slippers."

Omega gazed at the furred shabby articles on her bird legs. The water took time to pour owing to the furred spout. Aunt took down two cups.

"Thank you, Aunt. And one for Ome. Shall I pour one for you?"

She handed me a tin. When I got it open, a wood louse crawled out. Omega was too hungry to care, dipping a moldy biscuit into her tea.

Aunt glanced into a cracked piece of mirror, like Eileen, concerned about faces. Her mouth under the wrinkled overlip was dark scarlet. She took an old puff, dabbing her neck, looking better for the tea. I heard a radio next door. "Oh, you must have been a beautiful baby, you must have been a wonderful child." I repeated that I'd tell my mother she was alive and well.

"Write? Look, I've got a visitor. He's coming. I don't like Nosy Parkers. Why've you come?"

"Eeeh. Don't be like that, Auntie."

"I thought you might be pleased. We'll go now."

"What's it? I thought a lot of your mother . . . once. My . . . sister."

"Why did you leave Eileen with us?"

"Families should stay friends, Auntie. Eve is my best pal."

"My mother and my father will be pleased to know."

"What's it? Who?"

"My mother. And my father too."

"Him. Don't speak of him. He'll want to hear nothing. Him."

"Why, Auntie? What did he do wrong?"

"What happened to you, Aunt?"

"He's trouble. Him."

"He's strange. Not nice. He's lazy in his ways, I know that, Aunt."

"Not lazy in all ways."

"What do you mean, Aunt?"

"Not lazy about doing me. And anyone he could."

"Eeeh, Auntie. What a thing to say."

"Go on, Aunt. Please."

"Nothing more to say. He put me up the pole. Your Eileen is his child. Not long after your mother had you."

"Aunt . . ."

180

"Eeeh."

"What's it?"

"That makes Eileen my . . . sister . . . half-sister . . . cousin."

"Is it true, Aunt?"

"Cousin. Sister. True."

"Eeeh, Auntie. What a bad gent. Arab. Liar."

"You calling me a liar? Bad blood. You got bad blood, Eve. Here, that's my bell. Hear it?"

"I'll open it for you, Auntie. *Eeeh,* the Arab."

"Say it isn't true, Aunt."

"Why've you come?"

The bell croaked again. Omega put down her mushy biscuit sadly, excitedly. Sad that I'd had a shock. Excited that it was so interesting. I'd learned something to make me hate my people more. I might stay now, work with her on the corn plasters.

Aunt pushed me toward the door. An old man stood there wearing a ripped raincoat. She took him into the front room, closing the door, not speaking again to me.

Icy rain was lashing the street. Omega didn't notice. Sad, elated, awed. We'd not forget Auntie, would we? Poor little Irish lady. She raised her black cheeks to the sleet, singing the song we'd heard on the radio. Fresh air before we went under the ground again. Stepney was all right. We'd been lucky, hadn't been raped by an escaped prisoner or robbed. Hope we'd see no more ill pigeons underground. We'd had tea and a biscuit. "Oh, you must have been a beautiful baby. 'Cos, honey, look at you now."

181

So I knew. I understood about Eileen. Old goat, mad bugger, was her own father. Eileen that I'd followed, running from home to the metropolis, was my own sister. How many knew about it? Did the whole village, headed by Miss Taylor, know the truth? And my mother, who not only had the sorrow of Maxie but whose worn hands had the caring of him, her patient years lightened only by her giggling fits, did she know? I would tell no one that I knew, I would tell no one what had happened to me. The mad bugger that I'd cursed would live unpunished. Eileen, cause of pursed lips and head-shaking, had the blood in her, bore the same stigma. I hoped that she'd never meet her mother, dyed, downcast, bony, who had nothing to offer anyone. Yet once she must have had wiles, cajolery, have charmed the goat to his disastrous activity. Eileen, cousin, half-sister, blood of my blood, you're gone, our thread is snapped. Our mad bugger with the busted tooth was responsible. I should have run from your husband, who never really loved me. The long arm of coincidence outreached itself. What Matthew saw in me was duplicated in you. He forgot me until he passed the perfumery. Your horrid mother spoke. There's nothing here but sorrow, I will go back to the city. We're disunited. The past is unalterable, but I've learned. I'll grow, learn from experience, make use of my learning. No man is an island. Relationships are difficult, I'll make more friends. Omega will stay my friend.

Omega stood waving on the platform, not crying, keeping her face bright until I left. We kissed and I wept inside. She'd learned some confidence, she'd start on her own way, learn her own kind of relating, make some friends in the corn department. She'd learned that crying into a breakfast plate is futile.

Omega, I miss your black face, your woolly hair, your lime-oil smell. One day you'll be dulally over your own boy. May you be lucky. I wept over the paper flower that you made secretly, a farewell present for me, thrown at me before the train left, keeping your face brave. The petals, twisted cunningly, stayed stiff, cold in my hand, a gift of love made by your warty fingers. I'd nothing, no exchange. A kiss and the train moved. I leaned out then, my green gloves, wool for your hands, my gift to warm you, wear them to remember. I waved till you were a black speck, a friend, staying true and unalterable despite distance. I thought of you, my black metropolis friend, until the train reached Wales.

The sea was flat, I'd taken travel pills unnecessarily, the calmest leaving after the roughest arriving. Smooth, calm, with no wind, no rain, and no Omega. We promised each other to write. Writing spans loneliness, a letter keeps the thread. I've always looked for letters, friends should write letters. I number my friends on my one hand. Skin, true love, Mrs. Carter, Omega. Mr. Canner was a friend, set in his loneliness. The lonely heart sets like a mold, harder to break with years, acute in crowded places, dragging uncomfortably. Luck and endurance can change it.

I didn't sleep on the calm sea, I thought of friends who'd shown kindness, those who had not. The happiest times were with Eileen before we grew up. I will remember Omega. There is Skin to look forward to. Mrs. Carter will give me welcome. I don't believe Eileen or I will have children. They must never meet. I'd like to share my life with the one I hope for. A calm sea is an augury. If Mrs. Carter isn't there I'll take a taxi. I enjoy taxis. I've read of the sentiment of the Irish returning back, but I'm empty.

I knew that she would not be there. Taxi.

I called through her keyhole. "Mrs. Carter, here I am. I took a cab. I hoped you might be there."

"Glory be. I slept it out. I meant to welcome you on the quay. I'm jaded, worn out as per usual."

"What happened? Where are the schoolies?"

"Up in the bed. Work and more work. The showroom people are getting fussy. Fussy over a speck of dirt. They want hard scrubbing if you please, and punctuality. I'm jaded. 'I'm not young,' I said, 'I'm at a certain age. Nor am I a horse to do the work of two.' They didn't replace you. You can have back the job. Ah, girl, you're welcome."

"I'm glad. I'm glad to be back here."

Back again at the Carters', kissing her metal curlers while she looked shy. The Carters kept their kisses for those at funerals, or Dympna, but she liked it, I could tell. How had I got on over the water? Liked it, had I? Made a few friends?

"It was all right. One friend. A black girl, Omega. Why did you not write?"

"Black? A black girl, did you say? What name was it?"

"Omega. She got called Ome mostly. It's Greek. I wish you'd written."

"Greek? Heathenish. I did write from the show-rooms. I'm not great on writing, it's my eyes. You did say black? What country, Greece? You can forget her now."

"Her family came from Jamaica. She was raised in Manchester. Shall I wake the schoolies?"

"Leave them. Too late for school now. And forget nigger girls. Did you meet no English fellow, someone in the romantic line?"

"No one romantic, no. How is Dympna?"

"Great. A boy in the Mental has a notion for our Dympna, a bit of a romance there."

"And my hen? How is Biddy?"

"Ah, the birdeen. She is gone to God. God took her, Eve."

"I guessed it. What word from the hospital? How is Skin?"

The name I most wanted to hear of and I left him last. I had been false.

"Good news. He's after sitting himself up. Talking. Not a lot, mind, but he's much improved. The accident knocked a few feathers out of him, but he'll be up and about, especially now that you're back. How black is your friend? Very black?"

"Rather. She is my best friend."

"Your best? What about myself and C. Him? Are we not friends? You'll have to mix more, how will you tele-phone anyone from the showrooms without having friends? I think our Dympna may wed yet. I saw white in her cup, a veil or a shoe. The two of youse could have a double wedding when Skin is cured in himself."

"We never spoke of marriage. Not yet."

"You will. You will. Here, have a fag."

She'd heard that I had no bloke, she'd heard that Omega was truly black, she wanted no more news about England. She made no mention of her lads over the water. England, pagan, black, would swallow people if you didn't take precaution. Not that she had anything against a black skin, but what would a white Catholic have to say to one, what could you share? Was it true about dog food, that they put it in sandwiches? Where were my gloves? Had I some new clothes in that case, gadabout English ones?

I put Omega's flower on the Carter sideboard under the holy picture, pleased to be back there. The spring was coming. The city was warmer. The green buses, green postboxes, green telephone kiosks were as welcome as green buds. Here the people smiled again, interested in the discussion of weather, health, and religion, concerned with the state of crops and bacon prices. Church bells chimed. Clothes were oldfashioned. I'd bought little things, a knitted wool tea cozy for Mrs. Carter, who thought it was a hat, sweets for the schoolies, and a pipe.

The schoolies came down, showing their black teeth at me, kicking at their gym shoes with gladness. While I explained to Mrs. Carter that Omega was a civilized and humane person the schoolies found her paper flower. They took it into a corner to inspect it quietly and soon a shower of paper petals rained onto us. Mrs. Carter hit out at them. So Omega's present was gone. Flowers, both real and paper, died or disintegrated, loyalty stayed with you. I wanted Mrs. Carter to understand Omega. I wanted to keep the schoolies' friendship. The Carters cared deeply for each other, their own four walls were enough. The lads over the water, though rarely mentioned, had only to return and they'd be one, included in the circle as if they'd not left it.

Mrs. Carter said they'd celebrate my homecoming wth a good tea. She'd fry potatoes, make a nice bread pudding after. In the excitement of return, currants got spilled among the paper petals, got kicked into corners by the gym shoes. Omega, I'd like you to be here, you would enjoy it.

C. Him came in, charmed with his brier pipe. He'd got work now with the refuse disposal department, had left plastering in favor of rubbish dumping. Dustmen's work interested him, how did they go about it in the metropolis? Weekly or biweekly collections? He'd heard that daily collections were the coming thing, with free bins and supplies of refuse bags to householders, was it true? The schoolies shoved their food as they ate, kicked at each other, then settled to flicking breadpudding pellets. We had tinned milk in our tea and smoked a lot. Butt ends were saved for the schoolies to make roll-ups.

"You'll be visiting your financey, will you?"

"I rang the hospital before I came. I wrote from the other side, for news of him."

"He has been moved, he's in another ward. Not in the intensive now. Glory be, will I ever forget that night, the beast and the bad weather?"

"I know, they told me. He's in Vain's ward."

"A girl for letter writing. Sorry I never wrote."

"I hope Omega writes."

Mrs. Carter scraped plates into a newspaper. Never mind letters from friends with black skin who ate dog food. Forget over the water. I was too thin, that's what my traveling did. Forget Omega, life moved on. She'd tell them at the showrooms that I'd like the job back.

I'd expected a changed Skin. Ill for six months, having been near death, cared for intensively, would leave a mark on him. I'd expected he would be thin. He was emaciated. He sat by his bed. I saw his back first, the vertebrae a row of knobs under the gown. His hair hung long under his bony skull. His nose looked longer. His body was a long piece of string, easily snapped. He sat, trying to feed himself, lifting the spoon as if it were weighted. I had been treacherous, leaving him, forgetting him, I had been faithless. Once I'd seen Matthew again I didn't think of Skin, who was good to me, loved me. The sight of him tormented my heart. I wished I could erase time, take up where we'd parted, make him feel sound, the way he had cared for me, protect him. I'd disregarded, taken his unselfishness, left him. His spoon shook. He put it down. He looked down at his hands.

"You? So you're back."

"I'm back, Skin."

His knees shook under the blanket. The tray slid, spilling gravy over the plate edge. A potato rolled. His eyes looking up seemed inches large in his face, the sockets bluish. He was used to an open life, illness took a double toll. He blinked. His lashes seemed longer, blacker against the creased eyelid skin. His Adam's apple moved. His trembling made him seem nearly incapable. He smiled, though.

"So you did come back."

"I rang them. I told them. Didn't they say? Let me take that."

"They didn't say. I don't think they said. I knew that

188

you would come back. I don't remember. I was unconscious."

"I know. You were very ill."

Months of paralysis, he'd woken to be told I had left. Gone without a trace to another land on a capricious whim and no message. A sweat film spread on his upper lip. He was a poor color. The scar on his nostril deepened. But he smiled.

"I'm back, Skin. I will make it up to you."

"I know. I've no bitterness."

I wouldn't tell him that my journeying had been of little worth. I'd tell him nothing about Eileen's home, of Matthew, of Slough or Stepney. I'd tell him about Omega, tell of my one new friend, tell of the red buses, the cold, the strange faces. Speaking tired him. He lay back, eyes drooping. I took his fork, mashed the spilled potato into gravy, making it tasty, mixing the mince with the green beans, making a swallowable mixture. I'd nourish his thin bones, calm his ferocious trembling. He'd become handsome again, and quick-moving. I talked in a low voice, forgetting the ward round us. I had come back, I would take over. I'd do the worrying. I'd not prospered, I'd been disillusioned, but I'd toughened. I didn't hear the nurses, the other sick ones who discussed food, doctors' visits, the qualities of each nurse. I didn't hear the city noise outside, I felt and saw only Skin. I wanted to love him, sad for what I'd done. His opened mouth, putting the spoon in it was like feeding a thin bird. He stopped shaking then. He chewed the mouthfuls, keeping his dignity, not hurrying. The dinner smelled delicious. His feet in brown slippers were placed firmly now. And he smiled. He'd not enjoyed a meal since he'd come there.

"I'll soon be up properly. I'm getting independent. It's just weakness."

"I know. Have you pain? Where is the pain?"

"No pain. My spine is undamaged now. You're back and I'll be home."

"I shouldn't have. I thought . . . I got the idea that you wanted . . . that you said 'travel.' I didn't know what to do."

"And you were right. What could you have done here?"

He closed his eyes, weak again. A nurse looked watchful. She wanted no regression after his marked improvement. Time for bed. I could come often, come as much as I wished. Loved ones could help. She'd brought him ice cream but he hadn't touched it. The others had pie and custard, tapping their spoons, liking it. A moth fluttered against the light shade, drawn to it. Skin raised his eyes, half asleep.

"We . . . all . . . need . . . light."

The nurse gave me the tray to take, I could come back when he was in bed, after she'd drawn the curtains. Loved ones were often a tonic. I waited. I ate the ice cream a little shamedly. I asked the nurse if I could help her. I wanted to be the helper, caring and loving instead of eating his green ice cream. The moth made a little sound, hurling itself against the light.

"You can help tuck the corners. We're fussy about corners."

"I know. I've done it. I did it for my brother, folded corners."

"Oisin, you've an experienced visitor."

His clurichaun face was quiet on the pillow. And he smiled. "What happened to the bird?"

190

"She died. The Carters got rid of her. I'm staying with them."

His bed was neat, his dinner taken away. He slept. We would have other pets. When he was well we'd laugh and dance again. I longed to smother his greenish face with kisses, kiss the skin of his Adam's apple. The nurse told me to go. She'd been lenient, letting me stay after visiting hours, because I was a tonic and Oisin a favorite patient.

I left the big hospital. I'd go to the white flat, see what had happened, arrange and make plans for our lives when we came out.

The nurse had whispered how lucky Skin had been. A fraction inward, a hair closer, and Skin would have been maimed permanently by his kicking horse. I told her I'd come twice a day, his eyes, his thin hands, his trembling would respond, I would do anything she would allow.

I hurried to our old street. We would belong again, unite where we left off on the top landing, in the white attic rooms with the wiped picture of the Sacred Heart. I still tasted the ice cream, nut-flavored. His head on the pillow, alseep, had been beautifully angled, a portrait in repose. I would grow flowers for him.

The evening was warm. Citizens discussed the good stretch of weather, long light warm evenings heralded a fine summer. Good manners prevailed, their pleasant faces smiled if they bumped you. They were devout when passing churches, signing themselves or raising the hat, and no black face in sight. The landlord would be pleased to have Skin back, someone to collect rents again, keeping the stairs neat, smoothing the tenants' squabbles. We were an asset. I'd make arrangements

191

for the rent before going back to the Carters. I wanted to start cleaning, buying leaf mold, plants in readiness for his return. I'd move there right away, buy groceries and teach myself to cook. City sounds were music after the metropolis, the bells, soft voices, wagon wheels. I'd light a candle for Omega, that she'd not be lonely, find a good roommate, find a purpose.

The cracked wall of the tenement was all broken. Pieces of stone lay heaped everywhere. The house was a façade, the door was boarded up, the lower windows replaced with corrugated. Glass panes in the upper ones were smashed, the splinters littered among bricks. A great fissure ran down the brickwork from the eaves of the foundation. I looked up. It was gone. Our top floor, our attic rooms, weren't there. Plinths, girders stood dark against the sky. Tiles lay by the iron railings with the masonry, ready for haulage. The bins had already gone.

"What happened? Excuse me, please. Was there an earthquake?"

"Earthquake? The street is coming down is what happened. The city is changing, or haven't you heard? This is the first building. The street will come down."

"I lived here once."

"Not any more, God help you. Were you away? The occupants have been rehoused. The city is replanning. Where have you been? See the Dublin Corporation housing people about getting a place."

"Glory, girl. All the tenements in that area are due for demolition. I could have told you. You should go to the authorities. A maisonette would be grand, or a bungalow. A bung would be a lovely home. C. Him would love one, so would I. Stay here, girl. C. Him and the schoolies think the world of you, stay here for good."

"You haven't the room, Mrs. Carter. And Skin will soon be out."

After four weeks I was still upset by the ruined tenement, the disappearance of our white top floor. Mrs. Carter turned her tired eyes to the cup again, having completed her telephoning. We must both stay at their place, they'd find room. When would we be married? Where?

"As soon as we find a place. The church of the novenas if it's possible. I'd set my heart on the white flat, I cannot get over it."

"Away with the old, welcome the new. Forget it. If I were to elucidate. . . . The cup will tell us. The cup will show anything unusual, anything quare."

"What happened to Biddy? You never said, Mrs. Carter."

" 'Twas the schoolies. Ashamed of them I was,

shamed of my life. They got at the creature with sticks. She had stopped laying. The birdeen was unfit."

"You ate her? You ate my pet?"

Old times, old hopes and schemes, changed now. No white top flat, no flowers. Skin's gelding dead. Biddy entering a stew, along with pearl barley, masticated by the schoolies and Mrs. Carter looking mortified. Eileen, pretending Scottishness, married to a technician, aiming for stardom in the world of films. Bridie, whom I'd met accidentally in the street, engaged, wearing Damian's ring. She had paused long enough on teetering patent heels to describe the wedding celebration, champagne arrangements made by the Killems. Her gown was to be Paris-made, a chic affair on the whole. I could come along, to watch her walk into the church. Understand, invites were limited, Damian's family was large. But come and watch. Six bridesmaids, *naturellement*, dressed from the same French house. The yokels would yak for years. She didn't mention Eileen, or ask what I'd been doing. After the wedding they'd travel, a long honeymoon. *'Voir*. She'd smiled with sticky lips and waved her ring. Now all three of us had permanent laddos.

"You'll get another pet, girl. I've told you the truth. 'Twas but an old sick hen."

"I'm not blaming you. I'll miss her a little." I wouldn't forget her pecking custard, enjoying a cuddle, being danced, appearing to enjoy a pillow or a song.

Mrs. Carter said they'd make the front room over for me and my Skin, ready for when we got wed. Bridal, don't you fear, palatial by the time C. Him got his hands on it. Not for nothing had he learned plastering. She looked broodingly into my cup again. There was a veil all right, for me, not her Dympna. Dympna was

194

unready yet for marriage, her bloke was too much like herself. She looked momentarily heartsick. But she had me. She'd see me wed. I was the one the cup meant, I'd get the ring for my third finger and the white lace veil. Maybe Dympna was meant for a ring of another kind, a kind of bride of Christ. They took lay sisters for kitchen or washing work in the Mental, run by the nuns. She asked about Skin's work. Would he go back to the same employment?

"He's been doing occupational therapy. It's a miracle the way he has recovered."

"Occupational? What occupation might that be?"

"Painting. Woodworking. He wants to work with metal. He wants to make my ring."

I told her of his love of birds, his knowledge of them. Our home would have bird paintings, nightbirds especially. He planned a moonstone ring.

"Moonstone? What class of a stone is that? Girl, ask for a diamond."

"They're hard, glittery. I like something with warmth, translucent."

"A man in love will pay. Touch the heart and you touch the pocket. C. Him promised me the earth, though little enough I saw of it. His pocket can't stand the strain if I ask for sixpence now."

"Skin isn't like that. I'll not go short, not while he's alive. Or after, come to that."

He was provident, believing in insurance, the provision against mishap. He planned the biggest moonstone money could buy. We would be well suited. He was the only person to whom I could say anything. I wanted him to meet Omega.

"But work? What will he do?"

"He's going to study. Natural history. The social

195

worker at the hospital is helping him. He'll get state aid, a grant. I will work too. I expect he'll finish as a teacher."

"And chislers? How do you feel, are you in the same mind about chislers? They'd put an end to you working."

"I don't want them especially. I hate them rather. Skin's would be different."

"Girl, a chisler or two livens the home, once the moonshine has dulled. You'll see. Where would I be without my schoolies? The boys went over the water, Dympna is gone, I've still the schoolies though."

"I know. You love your own."

"They have their faults, nose-picking, doing for your hen with sticks and rudeness. C. Him and I would be the sorrier without them."

"We'll see."

"A proper-living Catholic wouldn't speak so. Not that I'm blaming, the church is hard, often asking for more than can be stood. If I were to . . . Glory, that quare brown horse certainly changed your life. I'm fond of animals and a bit of nature."

"He's set on study. He always has studied. The social worker says he'll go far. He has savings. We want to buy a place."

"Who are his people? Has he an educated class of a background? Teaching folk? That was a quare class of job he did earlier."

"No. He once lived with tinkers. They took him along when his parents went. They like an extra few children. He was unhappy, never fitted, felt he belonged nowhere. He set up in the trade he knew, studied whenever possible. He wanted to own a travel agency. That's changed now he's met me. I love him deeply."

"You'll need to, girl. Marriage. . . . If I. . . . He has a strange air about him. I give it my approval. You aren't the usual sort, no more is he. He thinks a lot of you. I wish C. Him were half as nice."

"If . . . Perhaps we could stay here till we find a home. We want to be married soon. He'll stay with his landlord till the wedding day."

Mrs. Carter coughed into her smoke. "Be sure. Be very sure, girl."

"I am sure. Life is beginning now."

"It's settled then. I'll make another pot, we'll drink on that."

The Carter front room had never been much used, the rare funeral or Christmas in the old days. Stacked now with old furniture, the room would be transformed by C. Him. A coat of whitewash for the walls and ceiling and we'd not know it, a grand little home to start out in. My fresh tea leaves had something the shape of a splash, imagine, a big splash. Ink could it be, or some of that whitewash C. Him used? A drop of ink added to whitewash gave it a tone, not quite so blinding. Come to think again, the splash might well be a bouquet. A bouquet for a bride. What flowers did I intend having? What would I wear? A bride in the home would be a big event. The schoolies would be over the moon.

"They can be bridesmaids. Would they like that?"

"They would. Oh, they would."

Mrs. Carter looked pink with emotion. It was so unexpected. She was my benefactress, it was a small sacrifice. Skin would agree, she'd taken me in, adopted me. The schoolies were quite welcome to walk in my wake.

I determined to have a dream dress, unimagined,

something cobwebby, ethereal. Mrs. Carter wanted to help choose it but I'd rather shop alone, at a little expensive shop. She nodded gravely; she understood, nothing in the twopenny class, I'd not want her along. I must let her know the color, she'd see to the schoolies' frocks. I told her I wanted white, but pink of the palest shade would look nice on the schoolies, that is if she liked it.

We'd marry in the church of the novenas, our first meeting place. We'd make our vows to a higher power, the life force greater than ourselves, the power that brought us together. We'd never part again. He looked forward to starting study seriously, fired by the social worker's enthusiasm. He told me to write home for my books, get back to the study habit whether I finished the course or not. I might register at a city college for evening classes if I wanted. Meanwhile the money he had saved would go on a down payment. He listed our name down with estate agents. Letters with lists of properties started arriving at the Carters'. The postman's visit was eventful for the Carters, they watched for him now. I didn't want a bung. Secretly I'd like a home near the Carters; friendly neighbors to start off with. We'd stay in their front room till we found our ideal.

The moonstone was lovelier than my dreams, translucent, set in gold. Not very bridal, not conventional, Mrs. Carter thought, but it did suit me. Nothing about either of us came near to the conventional but at least we were starting right, with the blessing of Mother Church. She didn't like to criticize, but what were my parents thinking of? Were they not concerned about who or where their daughter married? Not so much as a postcard from them. Had I done wrong? I told her there'd been family differences for some time, asking her quickly if Dympna would be allowed to come, to get off the subject of my background.

"It's unlikely. The Mental mightn't like her out on that day, not being a Thursday."

She looked wistful. She'd love to be a bride's mother. I'd never told her about Maxie. Both she and my mother had carried a cruel load. She said she understood, the chislers left, that was the end of it, like her own lads. Emigrants did that, they just went. The few prayers that she offered up were for her absent ones, the ones she couldn't see, that God would take care of them. She would provide chips in a bowl, hot sausages, and plenty of black porter. She'd make up for my parents.

I had never eaten off nice china. I bought plates, mugs, cups in sky blue and white with a delicate flower design. I bought an oak chest for our things. There was a big sofa in the Carter front room. You pulled and removed screws to turn it into a bed. With the bed opened the room was full, I couldn't get round it. The ink-tinted whitewash came off on my clothes if I brushed it. C. Him said that whitewash was cheap, no trouble to touch up, just take care not to scrape it. Skin and I saw the priest about the banns, looked into course prospectuses, looked for a house. Our home would be different, unlike anyone's. Mrs. Carter said that if my dress was to be secret she'd play the same game, the schoolies' frocks would be secret too.

By the time Skin was out of the hospital he had helped many patients less able, had taught them to read, paint, and to solve simple jigsaw puzzles. The social worker regretted his leaving, his potential was considerable. Those who trained late often did outstandingly. Energy, striving, could pay a surprising yield. I wouldn't let him see my dress either.

It was a fine day in early June. I made up our bed with new sheets, I'd never again make it for myself alone. The room looked neat and clean. Mrs. Carter gasped when she came in. The cobwebby dress was out of this world, it was entirely gorgeous, I was a fairy from fairyland. I settled the lace points of the sleeves over the backs of my hands. My moonstone shone, waiting for the new ring to go with it. The dress had a tight bodice. The full skirt clung as I moved, the petal-pointed hem brushing my calves. I wanted Omega to see me. She couldn't get away. She'd written that they were short-handed on the corns. A small wedding, just the Carters, with Skin's landlord for best man. My lovely life, my luck had started, I had it in my hand.

C. Him had hired a black moving van to take the household to the church, where Skin and his landlord waited. Each of us prepared happily, each one beautiful in his way. C. Him had brushed his suit, the shoulders shone from his effort (he being prone to dandruff). He'd shined the shoes of the family early. No gym shoes on anybody's feet today, no cracked leather without shoelaces. My own were soft and fine, dancer's shoes with flat heels.

I was prepared for the schoolies to look unusual, had braced myself. Their cerise velveteen dresses made them look like boiled sausages, the bright skin tight on their bodies. The scrimped armholes, the overlong sleeves doubled back at the wrists turned their arms into smaller sausages. Mrs. Carter had scrubbed them red raw, forgetting their black-rimmed nails in her ardor. Their nails matched their shoes and black stockings. They were topped with black berets, pulled over their faces. They smiled their blackened teeth at me, without malice today. They carried black prayer books, believing themselves beautiful. Mrs. Carter removed her metal curlers, winding the hair over a toque twisted from a showroom duster. She wore her usual coat, a feathered collar pinned over it. Cocksfeather tippets were all the thing, she assured me seriously. She'd got it in a market. She had on thick stockings over her mauve-veined legs.

I kept looking at myself, more lovely than my dreams, a midsummer dress for a midsummer marriage, with my hair falling naturally, after a herbal rinse. I was the proudest of brides sitting by C. Him in the black van. He was to give me away. Mrs. Carter controlled the schoolies in the back. Smoke from cigarettes wafted through the small window behind our heads, and giggling. From time to time a schoolie face would peer at me and C. Him. It was a big van, dark in the back but for the little window. Neighbors called from their doors as we drove by, slowly for their benefit. "May you have joy and peace." "God bless the day, and all who come after you." It was a proud day for the Carters. Mrs. Carter regretted that I had no flowers, nor veil for my head. Where was the veil in the cup? I picked some of the ox-eyed daisies growing in their yard, twining them into a crown.

Skin stood by the door of the church of the novenas, his old self again, though not tanned. He strained to see up and down the street, not expecting a furniture van. He was still thinner than the first time I'd seen him, standing on his cart behind the brown horse in the same place. Now I had the unusual vehicle.

"Get you back, Skin. Get into the church, you're asking for bad luck. You shouldn't see the bride. Glory, where is your best man? Get back."

"I must see Eve. I want to . . . ah, you're lovely, my dear one. You're beautiful. I wanted to . . ."

"Away inside with you. Did you see my chislers? Look at the pink."

Mrs. Carter gave him a shove, pushing him inside ahead of us. C. Him took my arm, holding himself proudly and straight. My own father should be doing it, my own father wouldn't or couldn't. C. Him would act gladly, a proud day for him. The schoolies hung back in the porch, shy suddenly, picking their noses agitatedly. No Carter was overfond of a church. The church was so strict and bossy.

"Inside with you. Glory, what is wrong?"

I noticed the smell at once, not a candle smell, not polish, not incense. I smelled the smell of grass, a leathery outdoor smell mixed with the smell of flesh. The church was packed with strangers. I stopped smiling. Who were the uninvited ones, a crowd of them? Could they be making a film? Had Eileen arranged something with a film crew, arranged a surprise? The church rustled with the whispering of highly colored strangers, all of them peering to watch.

"Glory, it's the gypsies. Gypsies have come to look at you, Eve. Glory be to the Lord God, what a wedding."

"Tinkers, look at the tinks." The schoolies lowered their fingers, astonished.

"Itinerants, that's what they call them. I-tin-er-ants. A set of chawbones."

C. Him brushed his shoulders, setting them firmly, walking me up the aisle, grasping my lace sleeve. Chawbones or no, he'd carry on. This was the Carters' day, itinerants wouldn't spoil it. He scowled back at the schoolies, who had started to sing softly: "My mother said that I never should play with the gypsies in the wood." It was my wedding march.

Skin stood stiffly by the side of his landlord. He'd tried to warn me when I got down from the van. Too late now, he hoped I didn't mind, hoped I wasn't disturbed by these unusual guests.

The priest looked flummoxed. All of God's children were welcome. Some were more welcome than others. It showed that his church was known to the travelers, else they'd not have come in such numbers. A particular feast day of theirs, a little-known one perhaps. A prayer and a word of thanks, a look at a parish wedding. A wedding made a good show.

"You don't mind, do you, my dear one? They must have been known by my guardian, word must have got round. I don't know one face here. They have ways of knowing. Say you don't mind."

"Why should I if you don't? I'm happy."

"You wanted a small wedding, I was worried."

"Everyone is out in their best. Look, Skin."

The clothes they wore were brighter than the schoolies'. A few had sprigs of heather, ready to sell in baskets, the stalks bound in tight foil. One held a box containing wooden clothespins. A few of the older women wore shawls, containing a child, tucked in. The youngsters were brightest of all, bright clashing colors, petunia and orange, violet with brilliant green. Their heads were greased, their eyes were bold, unblinking, staring, narrowed eyes, not unfriendly. The men looked less easy, not so comfortable there in the pews, their hands held awkwardly. There were a lot of children. My guests were nearly all gypsies, my music a chant from the schoolies. I'd be leaping over a fire next, in a circle of caravan wheels, nothing would surprise me.

But I was surprised further at the sight of Omega sitting between two familiar figures, there in the second pew.

"Omega, Ome, you came after all."

She rushed to me, tripping across a kneeler. She wore her limey two-piece, tighter than ever, and she smelled the same.

"I couldn't miss your wedding. *Eeeh,* Eve. I had to. I just left the corns and came. I've met your Mum and Dad."

I looked over her shoulder at my parents. I saw my father fingering his unused and dusty beads, removed from the dresser for the event. He didn't know what to do with them. He didn't look at me. His mouth was closed over his teeth, his moustache had had a good waxing. In front, on the pew in front of him, was a new trilby hat. My mother looked at me, heart in her eyes. She had on a hair net sewn with small sequins and a gray blouse. Her jaw was just as furry. Her face begged acceptance, love, but there was moisture in her eyes. She hadn't changed, it would not take much more to trigger off a laughing attack. Her own child's wedding and she not asked, naught but a mention in a letter about books. My guests were a bunch of demons, filling the church, stinking the place up, while a great black creature hugged and kissed me, a creature in limey yellow. Lord God Lord, why no invite for herself and Ab? Who were my legal parents if not herself and Ab? She'd no objection to the demons or that black creature with a London accent, they couldn't help their natures, hard cases all of them. She would have liked a chance, a chance to accept or refuse her own child's wedding service, a chance to tell Miss Taylor about it. I'd gone behind her back, a hole-and-corner party with demons and black creatures. She tried to straighten her lips, failed, raised her hanky to her eyes. Heathen heather, not a flower in sight except a few daisies on my head. Clothespins, Lord God Lord. Demons.

"Let us proceed. To your places, please. Now then, please."

The priest wore a begging expression, appealing to us, trying to be stern. Omega went back to the pew, to sit between my parents.

I found it hard to listen while he prayed over us, hard to keep my mind on the solemn vow. "I, Eve . . . take . . ." I looked up at the Sacred Heart, where I had prayed not so long ago, above the long thin candles, lighting the grave face. His beard appeared to wave, a friendly look, not cross now in the candle haze. I smelled the gypsy smell, a musky undertone, from oil possibly, to rub into their skin against the weather. I glanced behind me. I smelled Omega's lime oil and my mother's lavender. My nose was still keen, despite foreign travel. The heather made nice patches of color in the nave, pale amid the bright coloring of the guests, surrounded by the stations of the cross. "Home," "family," "love" were good words now. What would we do with them all afterward?

We walked over to the sacristy. Mrs. Carter darted after, she'd not let my parents forestall her, she'd witness, this was her moment, I was her child, this ceremony was her job. The gypsies were my luck, luck for the bride, she'd entertain the lot of them. She'd borrow cups, jam jars, anything, to toast the bridal pair. She settled her cocksfeather tippet, had a hurried conference with C. Him, who nodded agreement. A nice hooley in the Carter kitchen for all to enjoy, see it through in style. I had the man I wanted, man of my choice, I had my nigger friend from the metropolis, my Ma and Da up from the country. My man's friends and relatives, whoever they might be, itinerant or heathen were welcome as flowers in June. We'd all go back to the Carters'.

After we'd finished signing I kissed the faces near me, the Carters, Omega. I kissed Skin. Now I was flying, my wings were gossamer. Now we'd go down the aisle, officially man and wife. Now I would kiss my parents. The schoolies started to hum again, the same little rhyme. I stepped toward the second pew, there was a horrid groan, a kind of horrid croak as my father's bald pate tipped forward toward the pew in front. Relief, remorse, or pain had made him ill. He must sit down.

"Lord God Lord, it's the excitement." My mother's hand flew to her mouth. His daughter's wedding was too much for him.

"He's overdone his few drinks. That and those i-tin-er-ants."

C. Him moved over to lift my father's head from the trilby, into which it wedged as he had fallen. Too tight, it jammed across his eyebrows. Loosen his clothes. My mother stopped smiling when the groaning stopped. There was a hush. C. Him jerked his head toward Mrs. Carter. This wasn't how a wedding should be conducted, this wasn't in the plan. Those itinerants were intruders. Who was that black? That's what you got for cutting a daughter off, abandoning her. He'd not have let those chawbones past the city boundary, much less inside the church. They'd done a mischief. As like as not, they'd a hand in the old man's fit, them and their

206

mumbo-jumbo, and that black, what right had she to kiss as if she owned the bride? Pressing rubbery lips to a white face.

"They're all our guests. We must see Eve through."

Mrs. Carter's feathers ruffled with excitement as she bent over my father. It took Omega, C. Him, and her all their strength, with my mother fussing behind, to get my father on the pew, out straight. The schoolies waved their black-edged fingers about, one of them fanned him with a beret. My father lay quiet. Slowly, quietly, the tinkers left their pews, gathering in a half-circle. A woman held out a heather sprig. The priest bustled to the sacristy, thankful that the patient was conveniently near for the last rites. I knew when he didn't stir from the beret-waving that it was too late. Old bugger, mad goat, knickers down, it's all over. The verger hurried too. First aid. An ambulance.

"I knew it. Glory, didn't I see the veil in the cup. A shroud, I seen it. A shroud and a splash of something."

"People, it's too late. He's gone, and may he rest in peace. I've telephoned. They'll come for him."

The gypsies were crossing themselves with fervor by the time the priest had done splashing the holy water, having touched my father's forehead, lips, and chest with the oil, signing his genitals, cause of regret and sorrow. My mother keened. Having almost turned a somersault into his trilby hat, Abner had gone, was having his hands crossed suitably across his chest, stretched out on the pew where less than an hour earlier he'd watched me getting married. A gypsy granny took up the keening. He'd made no last confession, though the oil brought luck. No wafer passed his lips, though he'd died on good ground. White heather was a luck sign, dead or alive. The priest, an old man, was shaking. In all his years he'd not had a death hard on the heels of a wedding, right on holy premises. He found no fault with the strangers, they were exemplary, bowing the neck, sighing, showing respect for his cloth and the deceased body. Someone offered him a heather sprig, another touched his surplice. A lad chewed on a clothespin anxiously. Too late, the bride's real father had passed out.

My soft soles made no sound on the stone floor. I knelt by my father. Mad bugger, goat, forgive me. I cursed you, ran away, now I am married. I've my own husband, real and alive, nothing shall spoil the day, I forgive everything.

"People, leave it to me. He's had the rites. I'll see to it. Poor man. I've phoned Emergency."

My mother stayed silent, whispering "Lord," beaten, hands hanging, sad in the sepia light, almost extinct herself.

"They must have sustenance, the guests must have a glass." Itinerant chawbones or black, a thirst was common to nations.

"We can't send them away empty. Glory be to the Lord God, a quare wedding. Didn't I see the splash? We'll give them a good feed, make it up to them."

"Eeeh, Eve. I'm sorry. What can I do? Your Skin is enough to make anyone dulally."

"What can anyone do? I'm glad you're here, Omega."

My mother was a widow. It was still my day. My cheeks were wet, though.

"My dearling, my own Eve."

Skin pressed me to his chest, my face against his wedding tie. I knew then that he'd guessed. Something

208

had been dreadfully wrong at home, too late to be put right.

"Lord, Lord," whispered my mother. Was she blaming me for not asking my father to give me away, instead of the man with the dandruffy shoulders?

"The men will take him away. Make way there." The verger was in command. He must see that the priest sat down in the sacristy. Poor man of God, long past retiring, a shock the likes of this could trigger off another death. In charge, he poured water for anyone unsteady. Used to the bereaved, ready with a pat, a word of sympathy, a compassionate smile. Don't crowd my mother, give her time. A gypsy touched her. Darkened with trouble, snared in the teeth of grief, the barriers melted. An arm about you that understood erased racial or social differences. My mother must go with her man in the ambulance, stay near at his death, as she'd stayed near in life.

Silence and lowered heads as he was carried out. The schoolies were silent, scratching their heads under the berets. C. Him was more cheerful once my parents were out of the picture. He offered to ferry as many of the itinerants as wished back in his furniture van. Open house at the Carters' for the assembled company.

"Glory, I hope there's enough of sausages."

"*Eeeh.* Eve, what a sad thing."

"The van can make two trips. As many as you like, all welcome."

The tinkers were eager, leaping in a many-colored rush to the van doors. I sat on Skin's knee in the front, squashed in with the whole Carter family. My new ring felt smooth and lovely beside the big moonstone. C. Him could hardly reach the gears, hampered by the

209

cerise-velveteened limbs of his schoolies. We peered through into the dark back, just able to make out faces, and patches of white heather.

Back at the Carters' the strangers sat on floors and tables, every available surface. An elderly woman leaped up on a tallboy with a few children. A boy got on the stove, burning himself mildly. All of our backs became smeared with the whitewash from the walls of our parlor bedroom. They squatted on our bed with the new sheets, gay as rags. Though they were ragged they were clean, a washed and smiling assembly, appreciative of hot sausages washed down with black porter. Some huge potatoes were produced, hot from the oven, and a great cake. The schoolies gripped the potatoes in their black-rimmed nails, biting silently, the butter running down their chins. Neighbors arrived, drawn by curiosity, bringing more food, drawn by the fun. The half-gyppo wedding was an event the whole street would remember. Crates of beer arrived.

"We're clean. We're human like any of youse. You georgios think we're black dirty. We could show *you*."

The woman on the tallboy held a conversation with anyone who would hand her up a glass, but there were no speeches in view of the happening in the church. Skin held my hands, stroking, knowing I felt bewildered. Omega sat on the other side. I was in a dream state. Once, long ago, Skin had been one of these people. Who were my people now? Who were his? Someone brought in some rum. Soon Omega was sleeping, curled on the bed in a limey hunch. The schoolies had started chanting the gypsy rhyme again, when Dympna's great hat appeared round the door. The schoolies ran to her, hanging on her arms, handing her hot potatoes, handing her a glass. She was their heroine. Mrs.

Carter sat at the kitchen table, her cocksfeather tippet round her ankles, discussing the reading of tea leaves with some strangers. She was content. The kitchen was foggy with smoke.

C. Him got up unsteadily, brushing the dandruff away again.

"Friends and kin, owing to the misfortunate demise of Mr. Joyne the proceedings will close earlier than any of us would wish. I-tin-er-ants, I welcome you. I say goodbye hoping we'll meet again. Now we must say goodnight."

A bittersweet gathering, joy over a marriage mixing with grief for a departure. Skin and I thanked everyone as they filed outside. Soon the street was dark and quiet. There was silence inside and out. C. Him and Mrs. Carter went upstairs, Mrs. Carter tripping on her tippet before shutting their door. The schoolies crawled round collecting cigarette ends, enough for several roll-ups, before taking Dympna away, a night of happy whispering with her. I don't know if she understood. A wagon wheel squeaked far down the road. Skin looked at Omega, still curled up. The situation was perplexing.

"I think we ought to leave her, Skin. She will be left out otherwise. Let her sleep on."

A different kind of wedding, a different kind of wedding night, with Omega on our feet, a great bear of a weight. I thought I heard weeping once, in the early hours, but Omega slept on, deep in the world of sleep. Skin and I slept wrapped round each other. We had time, we had all our lives. I'd made a proper choice.

Skin and I felt that we wanted to be alone all our lives, encapsuled, sealed from the world inside our own egg. Mrs. Carter said make the most of it, love at that stage didn't last, make the most. We could have a primus stove if we liked, though she'd love it if we joined them in the kitchen. The schoolies liked lingering in the passage by our room, their gym shoes making a faint slither. They missed having me to tease in the bed and kick at. Skin was tolerant, he felt they needed attention, putting himself out to get them talking, buying them crayons, encouraging them to draw. I didn't like them listening at night. I didn't like Mrs. Carter snooping at our sheets. Skin said to bear with her, her life was hard. Circumscribed lives required outside stimuli, someone outside their daily round to wonder over. We'd be gone in a week or so, when we found someplace right.

We went to my father's funeral. His postmortem revealed nothing. An embolism from stress, the coroner said, having heard that there was no medical history, apart from bronchitic powders locally made. He went back in his box, to be laid out in Maxie's room, it being the most convenient. Skin insisted that I go. Who else had my own mother to lean on if not me? I would be needed.

212

Funerals and the bereaved were Miss Taylor's specialty, the day was a fine one, she was in her element. She provided trays of sticky sweet drinks, having arrived early to make the outhouse ready. She'd made a dark dress for my mother, like a habit. I looked at the priest, renowned once for his twisting, renowned for visiting the sick and parlor tricks. The dancing, the apple orchard days, were long ago. I was proud to introduce Skin to Miss Taylor, who said she'd known I would go far, marry a man with a fine future. There was barmbrack cake and sweet tea, and the sticky drinks. The port was extra sweet. Gone quiet since the death, my mother never smiled. Before the interment she took my hand, a rare gesture, said she was glad that Eileen and I got good men, that Ab had thought a lot of us. She stared bleakly at the heaped wreaths. Killem's sent the biggest. Ours was of anemones. I shed no tears except when I saw Mr. Canner. He stood apart, crying alone, his face in a grimace, crying for the grief that ought to have been mine. He came up afterward with a gift for me. He liked bottles, interestingly shaped, had quite a collection from the years. A pretty container to wink above our fire, a pretty bottle to remember him by. He said he always knew I'd catch the clouds, it just took courage.

Nobody mentioned Maxie. I thought Eileen might come, dressed to kill in black fur and a Rolls. As the cortege left the front gate by the fuchsia bush I heard the town taxi chugging. The London aunt, black as a crow, a scarf over her bright hair, stepped out. Respect for the departed, respect for her own sister, brought her from the metropolis. Sorrow was a great leveler, she thought she might be wanted. From respect she'd left her face unpainted. Those dry pale flaky lips had been kissed by the deceased. They kissed my mother now, who straightened herself up. A sister from her girlhood days to sit in the first car, a sister to lean on, made a difference. It helped to swell the mourners, it made another wreath. A few village children gathered along the road, and some outsiders. The cross old feller who cycled the hen-specked bike to the station was traveling in a box, his last journey, without cap or trouser clips.

Afterward the fat women held their glasses delicately, licking their lips, nothing escaping their notice. Skin nudged me, I must not pity myself.

"You are the only daughter, be proud, be dignified. Refill their glasses, welcome them. Be kind to Miss Taylor."

Aunt said afterward to leave my mother to her, she needed her sister. She would sleep with my mother, care for her.

Miss Taylor, Skin, and I cleared away. It had been a small funeral. I kissed Miss Taylor, who had stayed friendly through the years, making the shifts free, kind at the funeral.

"Is it all different from what you expected, Skin?"

"It is, my dear one, very different."

"This was my brother's room, you know. Ill all his life, until he went to the General. He'll be there always, I imagine."

"This was a fine place once. I can see that. We'll visit Maxie when we come again."

We walked out through the yard, all traces of the dye gone now. We walked under the apple tree. I told about lying there, watching the clouds through the blossoms, watching the shapes, waiting for a hen to fly up. Wasps buzzed now, in the weeds and grass. I showed him where the cockerel was buried, where once I had been kissed, the place where I'd been sick on the night of Maxie's grand fit. The hens were gone now, the hen-house roof had collapsed onto broken perches; no bike anymore.

"In London while you were so ill I got into . . . I didn't behave well."

"I don't need to hear, I don't want to. None of it matters now."

We stayed in the orchard talking. It was quiet. My calves brushed against nettles, he pulled up dock leaves, applying them to the bleeding scratches. I showed him the greenhouse corner, a few rusted spikes under the weeds. Aunt had taken my mother upstairs. It got dark. Skin said it was good that my parents had been happy before my father died, they'd been at peace, had known sunny days before the end. A pity the house was in such disrepair. The village was dismal, he agreed.

My mother looked better after her night's rest. I wasn't surprised when Aunt told me, having taken my mother her breakfast, that she was taking her back.

"And don't come worrying round Stepney, you or that man. And keep that black away. You make your mother worse."

"And Maxie? What about him?"

"What's it? She must get away. No need to sit in this cursed place."

My mother kissed me, a tear-sogged hulk of a woman. Was it imagination or did she have a twinkle? In Stepney, Aunt might influence her, get her to dye her hair, slim down and paint her face. My mother might teach Aunt to laugh.

Back in the city there was word about a grant, money for Skin's studies. Mrs. Carter was sitting at the table peering into the cup, looking for what she longed for, sign of a cradle or pram. Then came the letter with the Stepney postmark. "Dear Eve. I'm not returning. Do what you like with the place, it's yours."

Skin read it thoughtfully. Mrs. Carter asked to see it. Short, wasn't it, a terse note from my Mam. Glory, a place in the country. Read it again, would I?

So I am back here, where I started from, with Skin. Our baby is due in a few weeks. I visit the General each month to see Maxie, who is worse. A loglike patient, he shows no reaction, makes no sound, needing male nursing.

The old farm is becoming what a home should be, a place of light and welcome. Skin studies in the city, riding a motor bike to the station. We have hens again, brown ones. We plan to buy back the land, to keep a goat, bees even, and grow vegetables. We plan to have a lot of children. Mr. Cranner visits, drinking still but helping Skin in small ways with restoring the house. Each night and at weekends you hear tapping, sawing, planning, singing sometimes. I've heard Bridie is expecting too. She doesn't visit the Killems. One day I hope to read that Eileen is famous.

The outlying children stop now, talk. We found shamrocks in the orchard. If we work on our house and love it, Skin says our neighbors will do the same. Our front door does not stick. We have a proper kitchen. The blossoms are coming out. I've known the good, the bad, and the waiting times. I can survive anything with Skin. Next week Omega is coming to stay. *Mais oui, madame. Mais oui, madame, que vous avez un beau bébé.*

MORE
BEST-SELLING FICTION
FROM PINNACLE